In 1941 Isaac Asimov, founding father of modern science fiction, published a short story called 'Nightfall' which rapidly became a classic.

But 'Nightfall's' well-merited fame has always bugged Dr. Asimov.

As he reasonably says, thirty years of solid, star-studded* professionalism must surely have produced stories as fine as and possibly superior to that early tale. Nevertheless, there are still people around to tell him – and people whose opinions he respects – that 'Nightfall' is the finest thing he ever wrote.

Finally, in 1969, in an effort to lay 'Nightfall's' ghost once and for all, the author made his own selection of twenty stories from the scores he has written and presented them in chronological order in *Nightfall and other stories*. It became an immediate bestseller. For technical reasons this first paperback edition of *Nightfall and other stories* is published as two companion volumes (though each volume is a self-contained collection). This volume, *Nightfall One*, ranges from 'Nightfall' itself (1941) to 'C-Chute' (1951); its companion volume, *Nightfall Two*, (to be published later) covers the author's SF firmament from 'In a Good Cause – ' (1951) to 'Segregationist' (1967). They compose an unparalleled selection of the best of Asimov chosen by the author himself.

*Including the *Foundation* trilogy; *The Caves of Steel*; *I, Robot*, etc., etc.

D1471080

Also by Isaac Asimov in Panther Books

Nightfall Two
Foundation
Foundation and Empire
Second Foundation
I, Robot
The Rest of the Robots
The Martian Way
Earth is Room Enough
The Naked Sun
The End of Eternity
The Stars Like Dust
The Currents of Space
The Caves of Steel
Asimov's Mysteries

Isaac Asimov

Nightfall One

Science fiction stories

Panther

Granada Publishing Limited
Published in 1971 by Panther Books Ltd
Frogmore, St Albans, Herts, AL2 2NF
Reprinted 1972, 1973, 1974

Nightfall One includes the first five stories
published by Rapp & Whiting in *Nightfall and
other Stories*, 1970
Copyright © Isaac Asimov 1969
Made and printed in Great Britain by
C. Nicholls & Company Ltd
The Philips Park Press, Manchester
Set in Linotype Plantin

to John W. Campbell Jr.
for making 'Nightfall' possible,
and for thirty years of friendship
and
to the memory of Anthony Boucher
and Groff Conklin

Contents

The writing of 'Nightfall' was a watershed in my professional career. When I wrote it, I had just turned twenty-one. I had been writing professionally (in the sense that I was submitting my stories to magazines and occasionally selling them) for two and a half years, but had created no tidal wave. I had published about a dozen stories and had failed to sell a dozen others.

Then John W. Campbell, Jr., the editor of Astounding Science Fiction, showed me the Emerson quotation that starts 'Nightfall'. We discussed it, then I went home and, over the course of the next few weeks, wrote the story.

Now let's get something straight. I didn't write that story any differently from the way I had written my earlier stories or, for that matter, from the way I wrote my later stories. As far as writing is concerned, I am a complete and utter primitive. I have no formal training at all and to this very day I don't know How To Write.

I just write any old way it comes into my mind to write and just as fast as it comes into my mind.

And that's the way I wrote 'Nightfall'.

Mr. Campbell never sends letters of acceptance. He sends checks, instead, and very promptly, and that is an excellent way of handling the matter. I always found it thrilling. I received a check for 'Nightfall' but my initial pang of delight was almost instantly snuffed out by the fact that Mr. Campbell had made a mistake.

Standard payment at that time was a munificent 1¢ a word. (No complaints, folks; I was glad to get it.) The story was 12,000 words long and therefore I expected $120.00, but the check was for $150.00

I groaned. It would be so simple to cash the check and ask no questions, but the Ten Commandments, as preached to me by my stern and rockbound father, made it absolutely necessary to call Mr. Campbell at once and make arrangements for a new and smaller check.

It turned out there was no mistake. The story seemed so good to Mr. Campbell that he gave me a bonus of $\frac{1}{4}$¢ a word

I had never, till then, received so huge a payment for any story, and that was just the beginning. When the story appeared, it was given the lead position and the cover.

What's more, I was suddenly taken seriously and the world of science fiction became aware that I existed. As the years passed *in fact, it became evident that I had written a 'classic'. It has appeared in ten anthologies that I know of – including one British, one Dutch, one German, one Italian, and one Russian.*

I must say, though, that as time passed, I began to feel some irritation at being told, over and over again, that 'Nightfall' was my best story. It seemed to me, after all, that although I know no more about Writing now than I knew then, sheer practice should have made me more proficient, technically, with each year.

The thing has preyed on my mind, in fact, until the idea of this book came to me.

I have never included 'Nightfall' in any of my own collections of stories because it always seemed to me to have been so well anthologized that it must be familiar to all my readers. Yet perhaps that's not so. Most of my readers weren't even born when the story first appeared and perhaps many of them haven't seen the anthologies.

Besides, if it's my best story, then I want it in one of my own collections. I can also include other stories of mine that have proven successful in one way or another but have not appeared in any of my own collections.

So, with Doubleday's kind permission, I have prepared Nightfall and Other Stories, *with all the tales in the order of publication. 'Nightfall' itself is the first and now you can see for yourself how my writing has developed (or has failed to develop) with the years. Then you can decide for yourself why (or if) 'Nightfall' is better than the others.*

I don't know enough about Writing to be able to tell.

First appearance – Astounding Science Fiction, *September 1941. Copyright, 1941, by Street & Smith Publications, Inc.; copyright renewed, 1968, by Isaac Asimov.*

NIGHTFALL

> '*If the stars should appear one night in a thousand years, how would men believe and adore, and preserve for many generations the remembrance of the city of God?*'

EMERSON

Aton 77, director of Saro University, thrust out a belligerent lower lip and glared at the young newspaperman in a hot fury.

Theremon 762 took that fury in his stride. In his earlier days, when his now widely syndicated column was only a mad idea in a cub reporter's mind, he had specialized in 'impossible' interviews. It had cost him bruises, black eyes, and broken bones; but it had given him an ample supply of coolness and self-confidence.

So he lowered the outthrust hand that had been so pointedly ignored and calmly waited for the aged director to get over the worst. Astronomers were queer ducks, anyway, and if Aton's actions of the last two months meant anything, this same Aton was the queer-duckiest of the lot.

Aton 77 found his voice, and though it trembled with restrained emotion, the careful, somewhat pedantic phraseology, for which the famous astronomer was noted, did not abandon him.

'Sir,' he said, 'you display an infernal gall in coming to me with that impudent proposition of yours.'

The husky telephotographer of the Observatory, Beenay 25, thrust a tongue's tip across dry lips and interposed nervously, 'Now, sir, after all —'

The director turned to him and lifted a white eyebrow. 'Do not interfere, Beenay. I will credit you with good intentions in bringing this man here; but I will tolerate no insubordination now.'

Theremon decided it was time to take a part. 'Director Aton, if you'll let me finish what I started saying, I think —'

'I don't believe, young man,' retorted Aton, 'that anything you could say now would count much as compared with your daily columns of these last two months. You have led a vast newspaper campaign against the efforts of myself and my colleagues to organize the world against the menace which it is now too late to avert. You have done your best with your highly personal attacks to make the staff of this Observatory objects of ridicule.'

The director lifted a copy of the Saro City *Chronicle* from the table and shook it at Theremon furiously. 'Even a person of your well-known impudence should have hesitated before coming to me with a request that he be allowed to cover today's events for his paper. Of all newsmen, you!'

Aton dashed the newspaper to the floor, strode to the window, and clasped his arms behind his back.

'You may leave,' he snapped over his shoulder. He stared moodily out at the skyline where Gamma, the brightest of the planet's six suns, was setting. It had already faded and yellowed into the horizon mists, and Aton knew he would never see it again as a sane man.

He whirled. 'No, wait, come here!' He gestured peremptorily. 'I'll give you your story.'

The newsman had made no motion to leave, and now he approached the old man slowly. Aton gestured outward. 'Of the six suns, only Beta is left in the sky. Do you see it?'

The question was rather unnecessary. Beta was almost at zenith, its ruddy light flooding the landscape to an unusual orange as the brilliant rays of setting Gamma died. Beta was at aphelion. It was small; smaller than Theremon had ever seen it before, and for the moment it was undisputed ruler of Lagash's sky.

Lagash's own sun, Alpha, the one about which it revolved, was at the antipodes, as were the two distant companion pairs. The red dwarf Beta – Alpha's immediate companion – was alone, grimly alone.

Aton's upturned face flushed redly in the sunlight. 'In just under four hours,' he said, 'civilization, as we know it, comes to an end. It will do so because, as you see, Beta is the only sun in the sky.' He smiled grimly. 'Print that! There'll be no one to read it.'

'But if it turns out that four hours pass – and another four – and nothing happens?' asked Theremon softly.

'Don't let that worry you. Enough will happen.'

'Granted! And *still* – if nothing happens?'

For a second time, Beenay 25 spoke. 'Sir, I think you ought to listen to him.'

Theremon said, 'Put it to a vote, Director Aton.'

There was a stir among the remaining five members of the Observatory staff, who till now had maintained an attitude of wary neutrality.

'That,' stated Aton flatly, 'is not necessary.' He drew out his pocket watch. 'Since your good friend, Beenay, insists so urgently, I will give you five minutes. Talk away.'

'Good! Now, just what difference would it make if you allowed me to take down an eyewitness account of what's to come? If your prediction comes true, my presence won't hurt; for in that case my column would never be written. On the other hand, if nothing comes of it, you will just have to expect ridicule or worse. It would be wise to leave that ridicule to friendly hands.'

Aton snorted. 'Do you mean yours when you speak of friendly hands?'

'Certainly!' Theremon sat down and crossed his legs. 'My columns may have been a little rough, but I gave you people the benefit of the doubt every time. After all, this is not the century to preach "The end of the world is at hand" to Lagash. You have to understand that people don't believe the *Book of Revelations* anymore, and it annoys them to have scientists turn aboutface and tell us the Cultists are right after all –'

'No such thing, young man,' interrupted Aton. 'While a great deal of our data has been supplied us by the Cult, our results contain none of the Cult's mysticism. Facts are facts, and the Cult's so-called mythology *has* certain facts behind it. We've exposed them and ripped away their mystery. I assure you that the Cult hates us now worse than you do.'

'I don't hate you. I'm just trying to tell you that the public is in an ugly humor. They're angry.'

Aton twisted his mouth in derision. 'Let them be angry.'

'Yes, but what about tomorrow?'

'There'll be no tomorrow!'

'But if there is. Say that there is – just to see what happens. That anger might take shape into something serious. After all, you know, business has taken a nosedive these last two months. Investors don't really believe the world is coming to an end, but just the same they're being cagy with their money until it's all over. Johnny Public doesn't believe you, either, but the new spring furniture might just as well wait a few months – just to make sure.

'You see the point. Just as soon as this is all over, the business interests will be after your hide. They'll say that if crackpots – begging your pardon – can upset the country's prosperity any time they want, simply by making some cockeyed prediction – it's up to the planet to prevent them. The sparks will fly, sir.'

The director regarded the columnist sternly. 'And just what were you proposing to do to help the situation?'

'Well' – Theremon grinned – 'I was proposing to take charge of the publicity. I can handle things so that only the ridiculous side will show. It would be hard to stand, I admit, because I'd have to make you all out to be a bunch of gibbering idiots, but if I can get people laughing at you, they might forget to be angry. In return for that, all my publisher asks is an exclusive story.'

Beenay nodded and burst out, 'Sir, the rest of us think he's right. These last two months we've considered everything but the million-to-one chance that there is an error somewhere in our theory or in our calculations. We ought to take care of that, too.'

There was a murmur of agreement from the men grouped about the table, and Aton's expression became that of one who found his mouth full of something bitter and couldn't get rid of it.

'You may stay if you wish, then. You will kindly refrain, however, from hampering us in our duties in any way. You will also remember that I am in charge of all activities here, and in spite of your opinions as expressed in your columns, I will expect full co-operation and full respect –'

His hands were behind his back, and his wrinkled face thrust forward determinedly as he spoke. He might have continued indefinitely but for the intrusion of a new voice.

'Hello, hello, hello!' It came in a high tenor, and the plump cheeks of the newcomer expanded in a pleased smile. 'What's this morgue-like atmosphere about here? No one's losing his nerve, I hope.'

Aton started in consternation and said peevishly, 'Now what the devil are you doing here, Sheerin? I thought you were going to stay behind in the Hideout.'

Sheerin laughed and dropped his tubby figure into a chair. 'Hideout be blowed! The place bored me. I wanted to be here, where things are getting hot. Don't you suppose I have my share of curiosity? I want to see these Stars the Cultists are forever speaking about.' He rubbed his hands and added in a soberer tone, 'It's freezing outside. The wind's enough to hang icicles on your nose. Beta doesn't seem to give out any heat at all, at the distance it is.'

The white-haired director ground his teeth in sudden exasperation. 'Why do you go out of your way to do crazy things, Sheerin? What kind of good are you around here?'

'What kind of good am I around there?' Sheerin spread his palms in comical resignation. 'A psychologist isn't worth his salt in the Hideout. They need men of action and strong, healthy women that can breed children. Me? I'm a hundred pounds too heavy for a man of action, and I wouldn't be a success at breeding children. So why bother them with an extra mouth to feed? I feel better over here.'

Theremon seemed to see the columnist for the first time. He frowned and blew his ample cheeks out. 'And just who in Lagash are you, redhead?'

Aton compressed his lips and then muttered sullenly, 'That's Theremon 762, the newspaper fellow. I suppose you've heard of him.'

The columnist offered his hand. 'And, of course, you're Sheerin 501 of Saro University. I've heard of you.' Then he repeated, 'What is this Hideout, sir?'

'Well,' said Sheerin, 'we have managed to convince a few people of the validity of our prophecy of – er – doom, to be spectacular about it, and those few have taken proper measures. They consist mainly of the immediate members of the families of the Observatory staff, certain of the faculty of Saro University, and a few outsiders. Altogether, they number about three hundred, but three quarters are women and children.'

'I see! They're supposed to hide where the Darkness and the – er – Stars can't get at them, and then hold out when the rest of the world goes poof.'

'If they can. It won't be easy. With all of mankind insane, with the great cities going up in flames – environment will not be conducive to survival. But they have food, water, shelter, and weapons –'

'They've got more,' said Aton. 'They've got all our records, except for what we will collect today. Those records will mean everything to the next cycle, and *that's* what must survive. The rest can go hang.'

Theremon uttered a long, low whistle and sat brooding for

several minutes. The men about the table had brought out a multi-chess board and started a six-member game. Moves were made rapidly and in silence. All eyes bent in furious concentration on the board. Theremon watched them intently and then rose and approached Aton, who sat apart in whispered conversation with Sheerin.

'Listen,' he said, 'let's go somewhere where we won't bother the rest of the fellows. I want to ask some questions.'

The aged astronomer frowned sourly at him, but Sheerin chirped up, 'Certainly. It will do me good to talk. It always does. Aton was telling me about your ideas concerning world reaction to a failure of the prediction – and I agree with you. I read your column pretty regularly, by the way, and as a general thing I like your views.'

'Please, Sheerin,' growled Aton.

'Eh? Oh, all right. We'll go into the next room. It has softer chairs, anyway.'

There were softer chairs in the next room. There were also thick red curtains on the windows and a maroon carpet on the floor. With the bricky light of Beta pouring in, the general effect was one of dried blood.

Theremon shuddered. 'Say, I'd give ten credits for a decent dose of white light for just a second. I wish Gamma or Delta were in the sky.'

'What are your questions?' asked Aton. 'Please remember that our time is limited. In a little over an hour and a quarter we're going upstairs, and after that there will be no time for talk.'

'Well, here it is.' Theremon leaned back and folded his hands on his chest. 'You people seem so all-fired serious about this that I'm beginning to believe you. Would you mind explaining what it's all about?'

Aton exploded, 'Do you mean to sit there and tell me that you've been bombarding us with ridicule without even finding out what we've been trying to say?'

The columnist grinned sheepishly. 'It's not that bad, sir. I've got the general idea. You say there is going to be a world-wide Darkness in a few hours and that all mankind will go violently insane. What I want now is the science behind it.'

'No, you don't. No, you don't,' broke in Sheerin. 'If you ask Aton for that – supposing him to be in the mood to answer at all – he'll trot out pages of figures and volumes of graphs. You won't make head or tail of it. Now if you were to ask me, I could give you the layman's standpoint.'

'All right; I ask you.'

'Then first I'd like a drink.' He rubbed his hands and looked at Aton.

'Water?' grunted Aton.

'Don't be silly!'

'Don't you be silly. No alcohol today. It would be too easy to get my men drunk. I can't afford to tempt them.'

The psychologist grumbled wordlessly. He turned to Theremon, impaled him with his sharp eyes, and began.

'You realize, of course, that the history of civilization on Lagash displays a cyclic character – but I mean, *cyclic*!'

'I know,' replied Theremon cautiously, 'that that is the current archaeological theory. Has it been accepted as a fact?'

'Just about. In this last century it's been generally agreed upon. This cyclic character is – or rather, was – one of the great mysteries. We've located series of civilizations, nine of them definitely, and indications of others as well, all of which have reached heights comparable to our own, and all of which, without exception, were destroyed by fire at the very height of their culture.

'And no one could tell why. All centres of culture were thoroughly gutted by fire, with nothing left behind to give a hint as to the cause.'

Theremon was following closely. 'Wasn't there a Stone Age, too?'

'Probably, but as yet practically nothing is known of it, except that men of that age were little more than rather intelligent apes. We can forget about that.'

'I see. Go on!'

'There have been explanations of these recurrent catastrophes, all of a more or less fantastic nature. Some say that there are periodic rains of fire; some that Lagash passes through a sun every so often; some even wilder things. But there is one theory, quite different from all of these, that has been handed down over a period of centuries.'

'I know. You mean this myth of the "Stars" that the Cultists have in their *Book of Revelations*.'

'Exactly,' rejoined Sheerin with satisfaction. 'The Cultists said that every two thousand and fifty years Lagash entered a huge cave, so that all the suns disappeared, and there came *total dark-*

ness all over the world! And then, they say, things called Stars appeared, which robbed men of their souls and left them unreasoning brutes, so that they destroyed the civilization they themselves had built up. Of course they mix all this up with a lot of religio-mystic notions, but that's the central idea.'

There was a short pause in which Sheerin drew a long breath. 'And now we come to the Theory of Universal Gravitation.' He pronounced the phrase so that the capital letters sounded – and at that point Aton turned from the window, snorted loudly, and stalked out of the room.

The two stared after him, and Theremon said, 'What's wrong?'

'Nothing in particular,' replied Sheerin. 'Two of the men were due several hours ago and haven't shown up yet. He's terrifically short-handed, of course, because all but the really essential men have gone to the Hideout.'

'You don't think the two deserted, do you?'

'Who? Faro and Yimot? Of course not. Still, if they're not back within the hour, things would be a little sticky.' He got to his feet suddenly, and his eyes twinkled. 'Anyway, as long as Aton is gone –'

Tiptoeing to the nearest window, he squatted, and from the low window box beneath withdrew a bottle of red liquid that gurgled suggestively when he shook it.

'I *thought* Aton didn't know about this,' he remarked as he trotted back to the table. 'Here! We've only got one glass so, as the guest, you can have it. I'll keep the bottle.' And he filled the tiny cup with judicious care.

Theremon rose to protest, but Sheerin eyed him sternly. 'Respect your elders, young man.'

The newsman seated himself with a look of anguish on his face. 'Go ahead, then, you old villain.'

The psychologist's Adam's apple wobbled as the bottle upended, and then, with a satisfied grunt and a smack of the lips, he began again. 'But what do you know about gravitation?'

'Nothing, except that it is a very recent development, not too well established, and that the math is so hard that only twelve men in Lagash are supposed to understand it.'

'*Tcha*! Nonsense! Baloney! I can give you all the essential math in a sentence. The Law of Universal Gravitation states that there exists a cohesive force among all bodies of the universe, such that the amount of this force between any two given bodies is proportional to the product of their masses divided by the square of the distance between them.'

'Is that all?'

'That's enough! It took four hundred years to develop it.'

'Why that long? It sounded simple enough, the way you said it.'

'Because great laws are not divided by flashes of inspiration, whatever you may think. It usually takes the combined work of a world full of scientists over a period of centuries. After Genovi 41 discovered that Lagash rotated about the sun Alpha rather than vice versa – and that was four hundred years ago – astronomers have been working. The complex motions of the six suns were recorded and analyzed and unwoven. Theory after theory was advanced and revived and converted to something else. It was a devil of a job.'

Theremon nodded thoughtfully and held out his glass for more liquor. Sheerin grudgingly allowed a few ruby drops to leave the bottle.

'It was twenty years ago,' he continued after remoistening his own throat, 'that it was finally demonstrated that the Law of Universal Gravitation accounted exactly for the orbital motions of the six suns. It was a great triumph.'

Sheerin stood up and walked to the window, still clutching his bottle. 'And now we're getting to the point. In the last decade, the motions of Lagash about Alpha were computed according to gravity, and *it did not account for the orbit observed*; not even when all perturbations due to the other suns were included. Either the law was invalid, or there was another, as yet unknown, factor involved.'

Theremon joined Sheerin at the window and gazed out past the wooded slopes to where the spires of Saro City gleamed bloodily on the horizon. The newsman felt the tension of uncertainty grow within him as he cast a short glance at Beta. It glowered redly at zenith, dwarfed and evil.

'Go ahead, sir,' he said softly.

Sheerin replied, 'Astronomers stumbled about for years, each proposed theory more untenable than the one before – until Aton had the inspiration of calling in the Cult. The head of the Cult, Sor 5, had access to certain data that simplified the problem considerably. Aton set to work on a new track.

'What if there were another nonluminous planetary body such as Lagash? If there were, you know, it would shine only by reflected light, and if it were composed of bluish rock, as Lagash itself largely is, then, in the redness of the sky, the eternal blaze of the suns would make it invisible – drown it out completely.'

Theremon whistled. 'What a screwy idea!'

'You think *that's* screwy? Listen to this: Suppose this body rotated about Lagash at such a distance and in such an orbit and had such a mass that its attraction would exactly account for the deviations of Lagash's orbit from theory – do you know what would happen?'

The columnist shook his head.

'Well, sometimes this body would get in the way of a sun.' And Sheerin emptied what remained in the bottle at a draft.

'And it does, I suppose,' said Theremon flatly.

'Yes! But only one sun lies in its plane of revolution.' He jerked a thumb at the shrunken sun above. 'Beta! And it has been shown that the eclipse will occur only when the arrangement of the suns is such that Beta is alone in its hemisphere and at maximum distance, at which time the moon is invariable at minimum distance. The eclipse that results, with the moon seven times the apparent diameter of Beta, covers all of Lagash and lasts well over half a day, so that no spot on the planet escapes the effects. *That eclipse comes once every two thousand and forty-nine years.'*

Theremon's face was drawn into an expressionless mask. 'And that's my story?'

The psychologist nodded. 'That's all of it. First the eclipse – which will start in three quarters of an hour – then universal Darkness and, maybe, these mysterious Stars – then madness, and end of the cycle.'

He brooded. 'We had two months' leeway – we at the Observatory – and that wasn't enough time to persuade Lagash of the danger. Two centuries might not have been enough. But our records are at the Hideout, and today we photograph the eclipse. The next cycle will *start off* with the truth, and when the *next* eclipse comes, mankind will at last be ready for it. Come to think of it, that's part of your story too.'

A thin wind ruffled the curtains at the window as Theremon opened it and leaned out. It played coldly with his hair as he stared at the crimson sunlight on his hand. Then he turned in sudden rebellion.

'What is there in Darkness to drive *me* mad?'

Sheerin smiled to himself as he spun the empty liquor bottle with abstracted motions of his hand. 'Have you ever experienced Darkness, young man?'

The newsman leaned against the wall and considered. 'No. Can't say I have. But I know what it is. Just – uh –' He made vague motions with his fingers and then brightened. 'Just no light. Like in caves.'

'Have you ever been in a cave?'

'In a *cave*! Of course not!'

'I thought not. I tried last week – just to see – but I got out in a hurry. I went in until the mouth of the cave was just visible as a blur of light, with black everywhere else. I never thought a person my weight could run that fast.'

Theremon's lip curled. 'Well, if it comes to that, I guess I wouldn't have run if I had been there.'

The psychologist studied the young man with an annoyed frown.

'My, don't you talk big! I dare you to draw the curtain.'

Theremon looked his surprise and said, 'What for? If we had four or five suns out there, we might want to cut the light down a bit for comfort, but now we haven't enough light as it is.'

'That's the point. Just draw the curtain; then come here and sit down.'

'All right.' Theremon reached for the tasseled string and jerked. The red curtain slid across the wide window, the brass rings hissing their way along the crossbar, and a dusk-red shadow clamped down on the room.

Theremon's footsteps sounded hollowly in the silence as he made his way to the table, and then they stopped halfway. 'I can't see you, sir,' he whispered.

'Feel your way,' ordered Sheerin in a strained voice.

'But I can't see you, sir.' The newsman was breathing harshly. 'I can't see anything.'

'What did you expect?' came the grim reply. 'Come here and sit down!'

The footsteps sounded again, waveringly, approaching slowly. There was the sound of someone fumbling with a chair. Theremon's voice came thinly, 'Here I am. I feel ... *ulp* ... all right.'

'You like it, do you?'

'N – no. It's pretty awful. The walls seem to be –' He paused. 'They seem to be closing in on me. I keep wanting to push them away. But I'm not going *mad*! In fact, the feeling isn't as bad as it was.'

'All right. Draw the curtain back again.'

There were cautious footsteps through the dark, the rustle of Theremon's body against the curtain as he felt for the tassel, and then the triumphant *ro-o-osh* of the curtain slithering back. Red light flooded the room, and with a cry of joy Theremon looked up at the sun.

Sheerin wiped the moistness off his forehead with the back of a hand and said shakily, 'And that was just a dark room.'

'It can be stood,' said Theremon lightly.

'Yes, a dark room can. But were you at the Jonglor Centennial Exposition two years ago?'

'No, it so happens I never got around to it. Six thousand miles was just a bit too much to travel, even for the exposition.'

'Well, I was there. You remember hearing about the "Tunnel of Mystery" that broke all records in the amusement area – for the first month or so, anyway?'

'Yes. Wasn't there some fuss about it?'

'Very little. It was hushed up. You see, that Tunnel of Mystery was just a mile-long tunnel – with no lights. You got into a little open car and jolted along through Darkness for fifteen minutes. It was very popular – while it lasted.'

'Popular?'

'Certainly. There's a fascination in being frightened *when it's part of a game*. A baby is born with three instinctive fears: of loud noises, of falling, and of the absence of light. That's why it's considered so funny to jump at someone and shout "Boo!" That's why it's such fun to ride a roller coaster. And that's why that Tunnel of Mystery started cleaning up. People came out of that Darkness shaking, breathless, half dead with fear, but they kept on paying to get in.'

'Wait a while, I remember now. Some people came out dead, didn't they? There were rumors of that after it shut down.'

The psychologist snorted. 'Bah! Two or three died. That was nothing! They paid off the families of the dead ones and argued the Jonglor City Council into forgetting it. After all, they said, if people with weak hearts want to go through the tunnel, it was at their own risk – and besides, it wouldn't happen again. So they put a doctor in the front office and had every customer go through a physical examination before getting into the car. That actually *boosted* ticket sales.'

'Well, then?'

'But you see, there was something else. People sometimes came out in perfect order, except that they refused to go into buildings – any buildings; including palaces, mansions, apartment houses, tenements, cottages, huts, shacks, lean-tos, and tents.'

Theremon looked shocked. 'You mean they refused to come in out of the open? Where'd they sleep?'

'In the open.'

'They should have *forced* them inside.'

'Oh, they did, they did. Whereupon these people went into violent hysterics and did their best to bat their brains out against the nearest wall. Once you got them inside, you couldn't keep them there without a strait jacket or a heavy dose of tranquilizer.'

'They must have been crazy.'

'Which is exactly what they were. One person out of every ten who went into that tunnel came out that way. They called in the psychologists, and we did the only thing possible. We closed down the exhibit.' He spread his hands.

'What was the matter with these people?' asked Theremon finally.

'Essentially the same thing that was the matter with you when you thought the walls of the room were crushing in on you in the dark. There is a psychological term for mankind's instinctive fear of the absence of light. We call it "claustrophobia", because the lack of light is always tied up with enclosed places, so that fear of one is fear of the other. You see?"

'And those people of the tunnel?'

'Those people of the tunnel consisted of those unfortunates whose mentality did not quite possess the resiliency to overcome the claustrophobia that overtook them in the Darkness. Fifteen minutes without light is a long time; you only had two or three minutes, and I believe you were fairly upset.

'The people of the tunnel had what is called a "claustrophobic fixation". Their latent fear of Darkness and enclosed places had crystallized and become active, and, as far as we can tell, permanent. That's what fifteen minutes in the dark will do.'

There was a long silence, and Theremon's forehead wrinkled slowly into a frown. 'I don't believe it's that bad.'

'You mean you don't want to believe,' snapped Sheerin. 'You're afraid to believe. Look out the window!'

Theremon did so, and the psychologist continued without pausing. 'Imagine Darkness – everywhere. No light, as far as you can see. The houses, the trees, the fields, the earth, the sky – black! And Stars thrown in, for all I know – whatever *they* are. Can you conceive it?'

'Yes, I can,' declared Theremon truculently.

And Sheerin slammed his fist down upon the table in sudden passion. 'You lie! You can't conceive that. Your brain wasn't built for the conception any more than it was built for the conception of infinity or of eternity. You can only talk about it. A fraction of the reality upsets you, and when the real thing comes, your brain is going to be presented with the phenomenon outside its limits of comprehension. You will go mad, completely and permanently! There is no question of it!'

He added sadly, 'And another couple of millennia of painful struggle comes to nothing. Tomorrow there won't be a city standing unharmed in all Lagash.'

Theremon recovered part of his mental equilibrium. 'That doesn't follow. I still don't see that I can go loony just because there isn't a sun in the sky – but even if I did, and everyone else did, how does that harm the cities? Are we going to blow them down?'

But Sheerin was angry, too. 'If you were in Darkness, what would you want more than anything else: what would it be that every instinct would call for? Light, damn you, *light*!'

'Well?'

'And how would you get light?'

'I don't know,' said Theremon flatly.

'What's the *only* way to get light, short of a sun?'

'How should I know?'

They were standing face to face and nose to nose.

Sheerin said, 'You burn something, mister. Ever see a forest fire? Ever go camping and cook a stew over a wood fire? Heat isn't the only thing burning wood gives off, you know. It gives off light, and people know that. And when it's dark they want light, and they're going to *get* it.'

'So they burn wood?'

'So they burn whatever they can get. They've got to have light. They've got to burn something, and wood isn't handy – so they'll burn whatever is nearest. They'll have their light – and every center of habitation goes up in flames!'

Eyes held each other as though the whole matter were a personal affair of respective will powers, and then Theremon broke away wordlessly. His breathing was harsh and ragged, and he scarcely noted the sudden hubbub that came from the adjoining room behind the closed door.

Sheerin spoke, and it was with an effort that he made it sound matter-of-fact. 'I think I heard Yimot's voice. He and Faro are probably back. Let's go in and see what kept them.'

'Might as well!' muttered Theremon. He drew a long breath and seemed to shake himself. The tension was broken.

The room was in an uproar, with members of the staff clustering about two young men who were removing outer garments even as they parried the miscellany of questions being thrown at them.

Aton bustled through the crowd and faced the newcomers angrily. 'Do you realize that it's less than half an hour before deadline? Where have you two been?'

Faro 24 seated himself and rubbed his hands. His cheeks were red with the outdoor chill. 'Yimot and I have just finished carrying through a little crazy experiment of our own. We've been trying to see if we couldn't construct an arrangement by which we could simulate the appearance of Darkness and Stars so as to get an advance notion as to how it looked.'

There was a confused murmur from the listeners, and a sudden look of interest entered Aton's eyes. 'There wasn't anything said of this before. How did you go about it?'

'Well,' said Faro, 'the idea came to Yimot and myself long ago, and we've been working it out in our spare time. Yimot knew of a low one-story house down in the city with a domed roof – it had once been used as a museum, I think. Anyway, we bought it –'

'Where did you get the money?' interrupted Aton peremptorily.

'Our bank accounts,' grunted Yimot 70. 'It cost two thousand

credits.' Then, defensively, 'Well, what of it? Tomorrow, two
thousand credits will be two thousand pieces of paper. That's
all.'

'Sure,' agreed Faro. 'We bought the place and rigged it up with
black velvet from top to bottom so as to get as perfect a Darkness
as possible. Then we punched tiny holes in the ceiling and
through the roof and covered them with little metal caps, all of
which could be shoved aside simultaneously at the close of a
switch. At least we didn't do that part ourselves; we got a car-
penter and an electrician and some others – money didn't count.
The point was that we could get the light to shine through those
holes in the roof, so that we could get a starlike effect.'

Not a breath was drawn during the pause that followed. Aton
said stiffly, 'You had no right to make a private –'

Faro seemed abashed. 'I know, sir – but frankly, Yimot and I
thought the experiment was a little dangerous. If the effect really
worked, we half expected to go mad – from what Sheerin says
about all this, we thought that would be rather likely. We wanted
to take the risk ourselves. Of course if we found we could retain
sanity, it occurred to us that we might develop immunity to the
real thing, and then expose the rest of you in the same way. But
things didn't work out at all –'

'Why, what happened?'

It was Yimot who answered. 'We shut ourselves in and allowed
our eyes to get accustomed to the dark. It's an extremely creepy
feeling because the total Darkness makes you feel as if the walls
and ceiling are crushing in on you. But we got over that and
pulled the switch. The caps fell away and the roof glittered all
over with little dots of light –'

'Well?'

'Well – nothing. That was the whacky part of it. Nothing
happened. It was just a roof with holes in it, and that's just what
it looked like. We tried it over and over again – that's what kept
us so late – but there just isn't any effect at all.'

There followed a shocked silence, and all eyes turned to Sheerin, who sat motionless, mouth open.

Theremon was the first to speak. 'You know what this does to
this whole theory you've built up, Sheerin, don't you?' He was
grinning with relief.

But Sheerin raised his hand. 'Now wait a while. Just let me
think this through.' And then he snapped his fingers, and when

he lifted his head there was neither surprise nor uncertainty in his eyes. 'Of course –'

He never finished. From somewhere up above there sounded a sharp clang, and Beenay, starting to his feet, dashed up the stairs with a 'What the devil!'

The rest followed after.

Things happened quickly. Once up in the dome, Beenay cast one horrified glance at the shattered photographic plates and at the man bending over them; and then hurled himself fiercely at the intruder, getting a death grip on his throat. There was a wild threshing, and as others of the staff joined in, the stranger was swallowed up and smothered under the weight of half a dozen angry men.

Aton came up last, breathing heavily. 'Let him up!'

There was a reluctant unscrambling and the stranger, panting harshly, with his clothes torn and his forehead bruised, was hauled to his feet. He had a short yellow beard curled elaborately in the style affected by the Cultists.

Beenay shifted his hold to a collar grip and shook the man savagely. 'All right, rat, what's the idea? These plates –'

'I wasn't after *them*,' retorted the Cultist coldly. 'That was an accident.'

Beenay followed his glowering stare and snarled, 'I see. You were after the cameras themselves. The accident with the plates was a stroke of luck for you, then. If you had touched Snapping Bertha or any of the others, you would have died by slow torture. As it is –' He drew his fist back.

Aton grabbed his sleeve. 'Stop that! Let him go!'

The young technician wavered, and his arm dropped reluctantly. Aton pushed him aside and confronted the Cultist. 'You're Latimer, aren't you?'

The Cultist bowed stiffly and indicated the symbol upon his hip. 'I am Latimer 25, adjutant of the third class to his serenity, Sor 5.'

'And' – Aton's white eyebrows lifted – 'you were with his serenity when he visited me last week, weren't you?'

Latimer bowed a second time.

'Now, then, what do you want?'

'Nothing that you would give me of your own free will.'

'Sor 5 sent you, I suppose – or is this your own idea?'

'I won't answer that question.'

'Will there be any further visitors?'

'I won't answer that, either.'

Aton glanced at his timepiece and scowled. 'Now, man, what is it your master wants of me? I have fulfilled my end of the bargain.'

Latimer smiled faintly, but said nothing.

'I asked him', continued Aton angrily, 'for data only the Cult could supply, and it was given to me. For that, thank you. In return I promised to prove the essential truth of the creed of the Cult.'

'There was no need to prove that,' came the proud retort. 'It stands proven by the *Book of Revelations*.'

'For the handful that constitute the Cult, yes. Don't pretend to mistake my meaning. I offered to present scientific backing for your beliefs. And I did!'

The Cultist's eyes narrowed bitterly. 'Yes, you did – with a fox's subtlety, for your pretended explanation backed our beliefs, and at the same time removed all necessity for them. You made of the Darkness and of the Stars a natural phenomenon and removed all its real significance. That was blasphemy.'

'If so, the fault isn't mine. The facts exist. What can I do but state them?'

'Your "facts" are a fraud and a delusion.'

Aton stamped angrily. 'How do you know?'

And the answer came with the certainty of absolute faith. 'I know!'

The director purpled and Beenay whispered urgently. Aton waved him silent. 'And what does Sor 5 want us to do? He still thinks, I suppose, that in trying to warn the world to take measures against the menace of madness, we are placing innumerable souls in jeopardy. We aren't succeeding, if that means anything to him.'

'The attempt itself has done harm enough, and your vicious effort to gain information by means of your devilish instruments must be stopped. We obey the will of the Stars, and I only regret that my clumsiness prevented me from wrecking your infernal devices.'

'It wouldn't have done you too much good,' returned Aton. 'All our data, except for the direct evidence we intend collecting right now, is already safely cached and well beyond possibility of harm.' He smiled grimly. 'But that does not affect your present status as an attempted burglar and criminal.'

He turned to the men behind him. 'Someone call the police at Saro City.'

There was a cry of distaste from Sheerin. 'Damn it, Aton, what's wrong with you? There's no time for that. Here' – he bustled his way forward – 'let me handle this.'

Aton stared down his nose at the psychologist. 'This is not the time for your monkeyshines, Sheerin. Will you please let me handle this my own way? Right now you are a complete outsider here, and don't forget it.'

Sheerin's mouth twisted eloquently. 'Now why should we go to the impossible trouble of calling the police – with Beta's eclipse a matter of minutes from now – when this young man here is perfectly willing to pledge his word of honour to remain and cause no trouble whatsoever?'

The Cultist answered promptly, 'I will do no such thing. You're free to do what you want, but it's only fair to warn you that just as soon as I get my chance I'm going to finish what I came out here to do. If it's my word of honour you're relying on, you'd better call the police.'

Sheerin smiled in a friendly fashion. 'You're a determined cuss, aren't you? Well, I'll explain something. Do you see that young man at the window? He's a strong, husky fellow, quite handy with his fists, and he's an outsider besides. Once the eclipse starts there will be nothing for him to do except keep an eye on you. Besides him, there will be myself – a little too stout for active fisticuffs, but still able to help.'

'Well, what of it?' demanded Latimer frozenly.

'Listen and I'll tell you,' was the reply. 'Just as soon as the eclipse starts, we're going to take you, Theremon and I, and deposit you in a little closet with one door, to which is attached one giant lock, and no windows. You will remain there for the duration.'

'And afterward,' breathed Latimer fiercely, 'there'll be no one to let me out. I know as well as you do what the coming of the Stars means – I know it far better than you. With all your minds gone, you are not likely to free me. Suffocation or slow starvation, is it? About what I might have expected from a group of scientists. But I don't give my word. It's a matter of principle, and I won't discuss it further.'

Aton seemed perturbed. His faded eyes were troubled. 'Really, Sheerin, locking him —'

'Please!' Sheerin motioned him impatiently to silence. 'I don't think for a moment things will go that far. Latimer has just tried a clever little bluff, but I'm not a psychologist just because I like the sound of the word.' He grinned at the Cultist. 'Come now, you don't really think I'm trying anything as crude as slow star-vation. My dear Latimer, if I lock you in the closet, you are not going to see the Darkness, and you are not going to see the Stars. It does not take much knowledge of the fundamental creed of the Cult to realize that for you to be hidden from the Stars when they appear means the loss of your immortal soul. Now, I believe you to be an honorable man. I'll accept your word of honor to make no further effort to disrupt proceedings, if you'll offer it.'

A vein throbbed in Latimer's temple, and he seemed to shrink within himself as he said thickly, 'You have it!' And then he added with swift fury, 'But it is my consolation that you will all be damned for your deeds of today.' He turned on his heel and stalked to the high three-legged stool by the door.

Sheerin nodded to the columnist. 'Take a seat next to him, Theremon — just a formality. Hey, Theremon!'

But the newspaperman didn't move. He had gone pale to the lips. 'Look at that!' The finger he pointed toward the sky shook, and his voice was dry and cracked.

There was one simultaneous gasp as every eye followed the pointing finger and, for one breathless moment, he stared froz-enly.

Beta was chipped on one side!

The tiny bit of encroaching blackness was perhaps the width of a fingernail, but to the staring watchers it magnified itself into the crack of doom.

Only for a moment they watched, and after that there was a shrieking confusion that was of even shorter duration and which gave way to an orderly scurry of activity — each man at his pre-scribed job. At the crucial moment there was no time for emo-tion. The men were merely scientists with work to do. Even Aton had melted away.

Sheerin said prosaically, 'First contact must have been made fifteen minutes ago. A little early, but pretty good considering the uncertainties involved in the calculation.' He looked about

him and then tiptoed to Theremon, who still remained staring
out the window, and dragged him away gently.

'Aton is furious,' he whispered, 'so stay away. He missed first
contact on account of this fuss with Latimer, and if you get in
his way he'll have you thrown out the window.'

Theremon nodded shortly and sat down. Sheerin stared in
surprise at him.

'The devil, man,' he exclaimed, 'you're shaking.'

'Eh?' Theremon licked dry lips and then tried to smile. 'I don't
feel very well, and that's a fact.'

The psychologist's eyes hardened. 'You're not losing your
nerve?'

'No!' cried Theremon in a flash of indignation. 'Give me a
chance, will you? I haven't really believed this rigmarole – not
way down beneath, anyway – till just this minute. Give me a
chance to get used to the idea. You've been preparing yourself
for two months or more.'

'You're right, at that,' replied Sheerin thoughtfully. 'Listen!
Have you got a family – parents, wife, children?'

Theremon shook his head. 'You mean the Hideout, I suppose.
No, you don't have to worry about that. I have a sister, but she's
two thousand miles away. I don't even know her exact address.'

'Well, then, what about yourself? You've got time to get there,
and they're one short anyway, since I left. After all, you're not
needed here, and you'd make a darned fine addition –'

Theremon looked at the other wearily. 'You think I'm scared
stiff, don't you? Well, get this, mister, I'm a newspaperman and
I've been assigned to cover a story. I intend covering it.'

There was a faint smile on the psychologist's face. 'I see. Professional honor, is that it?'

'You might call it that. But, man, I'd give my right arm for
another bottle of that sockeroo juice even half the size of the one
you hogged. If ever a fellow needed a drink, I do.'

He broke off. Sheerin was nudging him violently. 'Do you
hear that? Listen!'

Theremon followed the motion of the other's chin and stared
at the Cultist, who, oblivious to all about him, faced the window,
a look of wild elation on his face, droning to himself the while in
singsong fashion.

'What's he saying?' whispered the columnist.

'He's quoting *Book of Revelations,* fifth chapter,' replied Sheerin. Then, urgently, 'Keep quiet and listen, I tell you.'

The Cultist's voice had risen in a sudden increase of fervor: ' "And it came to pass that in those days the Sun, Beta, held lone vigil in the sky for ever longer periods as the revolutions passed; until such time as for full half a revolution, it alone, shrunken and cold, shone down upon Lagash.

' "And men did assemble in the public squares and in the highways, there to debate and to marvel at the sight, for a strange depression had seized them. Their minds were troubled and their speech confused, for the souls of men awaited the coming of the Stars.

' "And in the city of Trigon, at high noon, Vendret 2 came forth and said unto the men of Trigon, 'Lo, ye sinners! Though ye scorn the ways of righteousness, yet will the time of reckoning come. Even now the Cave approaches to swallow Lagash; yea, and all it contains.'

' "And even as he spoke the lip of the Cave of Darkness passed the edge of Beta so that to all Lagash it was hidden from sight. Loud were the cries of men as it vanished, and great the fear of soul that fell upon them.

' "It came to pass that the Darkness of the Cave fell upon Lagash, and there was no light on all the surface of Lagash. Men were even as blinded, nor could one man see his neighbor, though he felt his breath upon his face.

' "And in this blackness there appeared the Stars, in countless numbers, and to the strains of music of such beauty that the very leaves of the trees cried out in wonder.

' "And in that moment the souls of men departed from them, and their abandoned bodies became even as beasts; yea, even as brutes of the wild; so that through the blackened streets of the cities of Lagash they prowled with wild cries.

' "From the Stars there then reached down the Heavenly Flame, and where it touched, the cities of Lagash flamed to utter destruction, so that of man and of the works of man nought remained.

' "Even then —" '

There was a subtle change in Latimer's tone. His eyes had not shifted, but somehow he had become aware of the absorbed attention of the other two. Easily, without pausing for breath, the timbre of his voice shifted and the syllables became more liquid.

Theremon, caught by surprise, stared. The words seemed on the border of familiarity. There was an elusive shift in the accent, a tiny change in the vowel stress; nothing more – yet Latimer had become thoroughly unintelligible.

Sheerin smiled slyly. 'He shifted to some old-cycle tongue, probably their traditional second cycle. That was the language in which the *Book of Revelations* was originally written, you know.'

'It doesn't matter; I've heard enough.' Theremon shoved his chair back and brushed his hair back with his hands that no longer shook. 'I feel much better now.'

'You do?' Sheerin seemed mildly surprised.

'I'll say I do. I had a bad case of jitters just a while back. Listening to you and your gravitation and seeing that eclipse start almost finished me. But this' – he jerked a contemptuous thumb at the yellow-bearded Cultist – '*this* is the sort of thing my nurse used to tell me. I've been laughing at that sort of thing all my life. I'm not going to let it scare me *now*.'

He drew a deep breath and said with a hectic gaiety, 'But if I expect to keep on the good side of myself, I'm going to turn my chair away from the window.'

Sheerin said, 'Yes, but you'd better talk lower. Aton just lifted his head out of that box he's got it stuck into and gave you a look that should have killed you.'

Theremon made a mouth. 'I forgot about the old fellow.' With elaborate care he turned the chair from the window, cast one distasteful look over his shoulder, and said, 'It has occurred to me that there must be considerable immunity against this Star madness.'

The psychologist did not answer immediately. Beta was past its zenith now, and the square of bloody sunlight that outlined the window upon the floor had lifted into Sheerin's lap. He stared at its dusky color thoughtfully and then bent and squinted into the sun itself.

The chip in its side had grown to a black encroachment that covered a third of Beta. He shuddered, and when he straightened once more his florid cheeks did not contain quite as much color as they had had previously.

With a smile that was almost apologetic, he reversed his chair also. 'There are probably two million people in Saro City that are all trying to join the Cult at once in one gigantic revival.' Then, ironically, 'The Cult is in for an hour of unexampled prosperity. I trust they'll make the most of it. Now, what was it you said?'

'Just this. How did the Cultists manage to keep the *Book of Revelations* going from cycle to cycle, and how on Lagash did it get written in the first place? There must have been some sort of immunity, for if everyone had gone mad, who would be left to write the book?'

Sheerin stared at his questioner ruefully. 'Well, now, young man, there isn't any eyewitness answer to that, but we've got a few damned good notions as to what happened. You see, there are three kinds of people who might remain relatively unaffected. First, the very few who don't see the Stars at all: the seriously retarded or those who drink themselves into a stupor at the beginning of the eclipse and remain so to the end. We leave them out – because they aren't really witnesses.

'Then there are children below six, to whom the world as a whole is too new and strange for them to be too frightened at Stars and Darkness. They would be just another item in an already surprising world. You see that, don't you?'

The other nodded doubtfully. 'I suppose so.'

'Lastly, there are those whose minds are too coarsely grained to be entirely toppled. The very insensitive would be scarcely affected – oh, such people as some of our older, work-broken peasants. Well, the children would have fugitive memories, and that, combined with the confused, incoherent babblings of the half-mad morons, formed the basis of the *Book of Revelations*.

'Naturally, the book was based, in the first place, on the testimony of those least qualified to serve as historians; that is, children and morons; and was probably edited and re-edited through the cycles.'

'Do you suppose', broke in Theremon, 'that they carried the book through the cycles the way we're planning on handing on the secret of gravitation?'

Sheerin shrugged. 'Perhaps, but their exact method is unimportant. They do it, somehow. The point I was getting at was that the book can't help but be a mass of distortion, even if it is based on fact. For instance, do you remember the experiment with the holes in the roof that Faro and Yimot tried – the one that didn't work?'

'Yes.'

'You know why it didn't w –' He stopped and rose in alarm, for Aton was approaching, his face a twisted mask of consternation. '*What's happened*?'

Aton drew him aside and Sheerin could feel the fingers on his elbow twitching.

'Not so loud!' Aton's voice was low and tortured. 'I've just gotten word from the Hideout on the private line.'

Sheerin broke in anxiously. 'They are in trouble?'

'Not *they*.' Aton stressed the pronoun significantly. 'They sealed themselves off just a while ago, and they're going to stay buried till day after tomorrow. They're safe. But the *city*, Sheerin – it's a shambles. You have no idea –' He was having difficulty in speaking.

'Well?' snapped Sheerin impatiently. 'What of it? It will get worse. What are you shaking about?' Then, suspiciously, 'How do you feel?'

Aton's eyes sparked angrily at the insinuation, and then faded to anxiety once more. 'You don't understand. The Cultists are active. They're rousing the people to storm the Observatory – promising them immediate entrance into grace, promising them salvation, promising them anything. What are we to do, Sheerin?'

Sheerin's head bent, and he stared in long abstraction at his toes. He tapped his chin with one knuckle, then looked up and said crisply, 'Do? What is there to do? Nothing at all. Do the men know of this?'

'No, of course not!'

'Good! Keep it that way. How long till totality?'

'Not quite an hour.'

'There's nothing to do but gamble. It will take time to organize any really formidable mob, and it will take more time to get them out here. We're a good five miles from the city –'

He glared out the window, down the slopes to where the farmed patches gave way to clumps of white houses in the suburbs; down to where the metropolis itself was a blur on the horizon – a mist in the waning blaze of Beta.

He repeated without turning, 'It will take time. Keep on working and pray that totality comes first.'

Beta was cut in half, the line of division pushing a slight concavity into the still-bright portion of the Sun. It was like a gigantic eyelid shutting slantwise over the light of a world.

The faint clatter of the room in which he stood faded into oblivion, and he sensed only the thick silence of the fields outside. The very insects seemed frightened mute. And things were dim.

He jumped at the voice in his ear. Theremon said, 'Is something wrong?'

'Eh? Er – no. Get back to the chair. We're in the way.' They slipped back to their corner, but the psychologist did not speak for a time. He lifted a finger and loosened his collar. He twisted his neck back and forth but found no relief. He looked up sudenly.

'Are you having any difficulty in breathing?'

The newspaperman opened his eyes wide and drew two or three long breaths. 'No. Why?'

'I looked out the window too long, I suppose. The dimness got me. Difficulty in breathing is one of the first symptoms of a claustrophobic attack.'

Theremon drew another long breath. 'Well, it hasn't got me yet. Say, here's another of the fellows.'

Beenay had interposed his bulk between the light and the pair in the corner, and Sheerin squinted up at him anxiously. 'Hello, Beenay.'

The astronomer shifted his weight to the other foot and smiled feebly. 'You won't mind if I sit down awhile and join in the talk? My cameras are set, and there's nothing to do till totality.' He paused and eyed the Cultist, who fifteen minutes earlier had drawn a small, skin-bound book from his sleeve and had been poring intently over it ever since. 'That rat hasn't been making trouble, has he?'

Sheerin shook his head. His shoulders were thrown back and he frowned his concentration as he forced himself to breathe regularly. He said, 'Have you had any trouble breathing, Beenay?'

Beenay sniffed the air in his turn. 'It doesn't seem stuffy to me.'

'A touch of claustrophobia,' explained Sheerin apologetically.

'Ohhh! It worked itself differently with me. I get the impres-

sion that my eyes are going back on me. Things seem to blur and
– well, nothing is clear. And it's cold, too.'

'Oh, it's cold, all right. That's no illusion.' Theremon grimaced. 'My toes feel as if I've been shipping them cross-country
in a refrigerating car.'

'What we need', put in Sheerin, 'is to keep our minds busy
with extraneous affairs. I was telling you a while ago, Theremon,
why Faro's experiments with the holes in the roof came to nothing.'

'You were just beginning,' replied Theremon. He encircled a
knee with both arms and nuzzled his chin against it.

'Well, as I started to say, they were misled by taking the *Book
of Revelations* literally. There probably wasn't any sense in at-
taching any physical significance to the Stars. It might be, you
know, that in the presence of total Darkness, the mind finds it
absolutely necessary to create light. This illusion of light might
be all the Stars there really are.'

'In other words,' interposed Theremon, 'you mean the Stars
are the results of the madness and not one of the causes. Then,
what good will Beenay's photographs be?'

'To prove that it is an illusion, maybe; or to prove the opposite; for all I know. Then again –'

But Beenay had drawn his chair closer, and there was an expression of sudden enthusiasm on his face. 'Say, I'm glad you
two got onto this subject.' His eyes narrowed and he lifted one
finger. 'I've been thinking about these Stars and I've got a really
cute notion. Of course it's strictly ocean foam, and I'm not trying to advance it seriously, but I think it's interesting. Do you
want to hear it?'

He seemed half reluctant, but Sheerin leaned back and said,
'Go ahead! I'm listening.'

'Well, then, supposing there were other suns in the universe.'
He broke off a little bashfully. 'I mean suns that are so far away
that they're too dim to see. It sounds as if I've been reading some
of that fantastic fiction, I suppose.'

'Not necessarily. Still, isn't that possibility eliminated by the
fact that, according to the Law of Gravitation, they would make
themselves evident by their attractive forces?'

'Not if they were far enough off,' rejoined Beenay, 'really far
off – maybe as much as four light years, or even more. We'd
never be able to detect perturbations then, because they'd be too

small. Say that there were a lot of suns that far off; a dozen or two maybe.'

Theremon whistled melodiously. 'What an idea for a good Sunday supplement article. Two dozen suns in a universe eight light years across. Wow! That would shrink our world into insignificance. The readers would eat it up.'

'Only an idea,' said Beenay with a grin, 'but you see the point. During an eclipse, these dozen suns would become visible because there'd be no *real* sunlight to drown them out. Since they're so far off, they'd appear small, like so many little marbles. Of course the Cultists talk of millions of Stars, but that's probably exaggeration. There just isn't any place in the universe you could put a million suns – unless they touch one another.'

Sheerin had listened with gradually increasing interest. 'You've hit something there, Beenay. And exaggeration is just exactly what would happen. Our minds, as you probably know, can't grasp directly any number higher than five; above that there is only the concept of "many". A dozen would become a million just like that. A damn good idea!'

'And I've got another cute little notion,' Beenay said. 'Have you ever thought what a simple problem gravitation would be if only you had a sufficiently simple system? Supposing you had a universe in which there was a planet with only one sun. The planet would travel in a perfect ellipse and the exact nature of the gravitational force would be so evident it could be accepted as an axiom. Astronomers on such a world would start off with gravity probably before they even invented the telescope. Naked-eye observation would be enough.'

'But would such a system be dynamically stable?' questioned Sheerin doubtfully.

'Sure! They call it the "one-and-one" case. It's been worked out mathematically, but it's the philosophical implications that interest me.'

'It's nice to think about,' admitted Sheerin, 'as a pretty abstraction – like a perfect gas, or absolute zero.'

'Of course,' continued Beenay, 'there's the catch that life would be impossible on such a planet. It wouldn't get enough heat and light, and if it rotated there would be total Darkness half of each day. You couldn't expect life – which is fundamentally dependent upon light – to develop under those conditions. Besides –'

Sheerin's chair went over backward as he sprang to his feet in a rude interruption. 'Aton's brought out the lights.'

Beenay said, 'Huh,' turned to stare, and then grinned halfway around his head in open relief.

There were half a dozen foot-long, inch-thick rods cradled in Aton's arms. He glared over them at the assembled staff members.

'Get back to work, all of you. Sheerin, come here and help me!'

Sheerin trotted to the older man's side and, one by one, in utter silence, the two adjusted the rods in makeshift metal holders suspended from the walls.

With the air of one carrying through the most sacred item of a religious ritual, Sheerin scraped a large, clumsy match into spluttering life and passed it to Aton, who carried the flame to the upper end of one of the rods.

It hesitated there awhile, playing futilely about the tip, until a sudden, crackling flare cast Aton's lined face into yellow highlights. He withdrew the match and a spontaneous cheer rattled the window.

The rod was topped by six inches of wavering flame! Methodically, the other rods were lighted, until six independent fires turned the rear of the room yellow.

The light was dim, dimmer even than the tenuous sunlight. The flames reeled crazily, giving birth to drunken, swaying shadows. The torches smoked devilishly and smelled like a bad day in the kitchen. But they emitted yellow light.

There was something about yellow light, after four hours of somber, dimming Beta. Even Latimer had lifted his eyes from his book and stared in wonder.

Sheerin warmed his hands at the nearest, regardless of the soot that gathered upon them in a fine, gray powder, and muttered ecstatically to himself. 'Beautiful! Beautiful! I never realized before what a wonderful color yellow is.'

But Theremon regarded the torches suspiciously. He wrinkled his nose at the rancid odor and said, 'What are those things?'

'Wood,' said Sheerin shortly.

'Oh, no, they're not. They aren't burning. The top inch is charred and the flame just keeps shooting up out of nothing.'

'That's the beauty of it. This is a really efficient artificial-light mechanism. We made a few hundred of them, but most went to

the Hideout, of course. You see' – he turned and wiped his blackened hands upon his handkerchief – 'you take the pithy core of
coarse water reeds, dry them thoroughly, and soak them in animal grease. Then you set fire to it and the grease burns, little by
little. These torches will burn for almost half an hour without
stopping. Ingenious, isn't it? It was developed by one of our own
young men at Saro University.'

After the momentary sensation, the dome had quieted. Latimer had carried his chair directly beneath a torch and continued
reading, lips moving in the monotonous recital of invocations
to the Stars. Beenay had drifted away to his cameras once more,
and Theremon seized the opportunity to add to his notes on the
article he was going to write for the Saro City *Chronicle* the next
day – a procedure he had been following for the last two hours
in a perfectly methodical, perfectly conscientious and, as he was
well aware, perfectly meaningless fashion.

But, as the gleam of amusement in Sheerin's eyes indicated,
careful note-taking occupied his mind with something other than
the fact that the sky was gradually turning a horrible deep
purple-red, as if it were one gigantic, freshly peeled beet; and so
it fulfilled its purpose.

The air grew, somehow, denser. Dusk, like a palpable entity,
entered the room, and the dancing circle of yellow light about
the torches etched itself into ever-sharper distinction against the
gathering grayness beyond. There was the odor of smoke and the
presence of little chuckling sounds that the torches made as they
burned; the soft pad of one of the men circling the table at
which he worked, on hesitant tiptoes; the occasional indrawn
breath of someone trying to retain composure in a world that
was retreating into the shadow.

It was Theremon who first heard the extraneous noise. It was
a vague, unorganized *impression* of sound that would have gone
unnoticed but for the dead silence that prevailed within the
dome.

The newsman sat upright and replaced his notebook. He held
his breath and listened; then, with considerable reluctance,
threaded his way between the solarscope and one of Beenay's
cameras and stood before the window.

The silence ripped to fragments at his startled shout: '*Sheerin!*'

Work stopped! The psychologist was at his side in a moment.

Aton joined him. Even Yimot 70, high in his little lean-back seat at the eyepiece of the gigantic solarscope, paused and looked downward.

Outside, Beta was a mere smoldering splinter, taking one last desperate look at Lagash. The eastern horizon, in the direction of the city, was lost in Darkness, and the road from Saro to the Observatory was a dull-red line bordered on both sides by wooded tracts, the trees of which had somehow lost individuality and merged into a continuous shadowy mass.

But it was the highway itself that held attention, for along it there surged another, and infinitely menacing, shadowy mass.

Aton cried in a cracked voice, 'The madmen from the city! They've come!'

'How long to totality?' demanded Sheerin.

'Fifteen minutes, but . . . but they'll be here in five.'

'Never mind, keep the men working. We'll hold them off. This place is built like a fortress. Aton, keep an eye on our young Cultist just for luck. Theremon, come with me.'

Sheerin was out the door, and Theremon was at his heels. The stairs stretched below them in tight, circular sweeps about the central shaft, fading into a dank and dreary grayness.

The first momentum of their rush had carried them fifty feet down, so that the dim, flickering yellow from the open door of the dome had disappeared and both above and below the same dusky shadow crushed in upon them.

Sheerin paused, and his pudgy hand clutched at his chest. His eyes bulged and his voice was a dry cough. 'I can't . . . breathe. . . . Go down . . . yourself. Close all doors –'

Theremon took a few downward steps, then turned. 'Wait! Can you hold out a minute?' He was panting himself. The air passed in and out his lungs like so much molasses, and there was a little germ of screeching panic in his mind at the thought of making his way into the mysterious Darkness by himself.

Theremon, after all, was afraid of the dark!

'Stay here,' he said. 'I'll be back in a second.' He dashed upward two steps at a time, heart pounding – not altogether from the exertion – tumbled into the dome and snatched a torch from its holder. It was foul-smelling, and the smoke smarted his eyes almost blind, but he clutched that torch as if he wanted to kiss it for joy, and its flame streamed backward as he hurtled down the stairs again.

Sheerin opened his eyes and moaned as Theremon bent over him. Theremon shook him roughly. 'All right, get a hold on yourself. We've got light.'

He held the torch at tiptoe height and, propping the tottering psychologist by an elbow, made his way downward in the middle of the protecting circle of illumination.

The offices on the ground floor still possessed what light there was, and Theremon felt the horror about him relax.

'Here,' he said brusquely, and passed the torch to Sheerin. 'You can hear *them* outside.'

And they could. Little scraps of hoarse, wordless shouts.

But Sheerin was right; the Observatory was built like a fortress. Erected in the last century, when the neo-Gavottian style of architecture was at its ugly height, it had been designed for stability and durability rather than for beauty.

The windows were protected by the grillwork of inch-thick iron bars sunk deep into the concrete sills. The walls were solid masonry that an earthquake couldn't have touched, and the main door was a huge oaken slab reinforced with iron. Theremon shot the bolts and they slid shut with a dull clang.

At the other end of the corridor, Sheerin cursed weakly. He pointed to the lock of the back door which had been neatly jemmied into uselessness.

'That must be how Latimer got in,' he said.

'Well, don't stand there,' cried Theremon impatiently. 'Help drag up the furniture – and keep that torch out of my eyes. The smoke's killing me.'

He slammed the heavy table up against the door as he spoke, and in two minutes had built a barricade which made up for what it lacked in beauty and symmetry by the sheer inertia of its massiveness.

Somewhere, dimly, far off, they could hear the battering of naked fists upon the door; and the screams and yells from outside had a sort of half reality.

That mob had set off from Saro City with only two things in mind: the attainment of Cultist salvation by the destruction of the Observatory, and a maddening fear that all but paralyzed them. There was no time to think of ground cars, or of weapons, or of leadership, or even of organization. They made for the Observatory on foot and assaulted it with bare hands.

And now that they were there, the last flash of Beta, the last ruby-red drop of flame, flickered feebly over a humanity that had left only stark, universal fear!

Theremon groaned, 'Let's get back to the dome!'

In the dome, only Yimot, at the solarscope, had kept his place. The rest were clustered about the cameras, and Beenay was giving his instructions in a hoarse, strained voice.

'Get it straight, all of you. I'm snapping Beta just before totality and changing the plate. That will leave one of you to each camera. You all know about . . . about times of exposure –'

There was a breathless murmur of agreement.

Beenay passed a hand over his eyes. 'Are the torches still burning? Never mind, I see them!' He was leaning hard against the back of a chair. 'Now remember, don't . . . don't try to look for good shots. Don't waste time trying to get t-two stars at a time in the scope field. One is enough. And . . . and if you feel yourself going, *get away from the camera.*'

At the door, Sheerin whispered to Theremon, 'Take me to Aton. I don't see him.'

The newsman did not answer immediately. The vague forms of the astronomers wavered and blurred, and the torches overhead had become only yellow splotches.

'It's dark,' he whimpered.

Sheerin held out his hand. 'Aton.' He stumbled forward. 'Aton!'

Theremon stepped after and seized his arm. 'Wait, I'll take you.' Somehow he made his way across the room. He closed his eyes against the Darkness and his mind against the chaos within it.

No one heard them or paid attention to them. Sheerin stumbled against the wall. 'Aton!'

The psychologist felt shaking hands touching him, then withdrawing, and a voice muttering, 'Is that you, Sheerin?'

'Aton!' He strove to breathe normally. 'Don't worry about the mob. The place will hold them off.'

Latimer, the Cultist, rose to his feet, and his face twisted in desperation. His word was pledged, and to break it would mean placing his soul in mortal peril. Yet that word had been forced from him and had not been given freely. The Stars would come soon! He could not stand by and allow – And yet his word was pledged.

Beenay's face was dimly flushed as it looked upward at Beta's last ray, and Latimer, seeing him bend over his camera, made his decision. His nails cut the flesh of his palms as he tensed himself.

He staggered crazily as he started his rush. There was nothing before him but shadows; the very floor beneath his feet lacked substance. And then someone was upon him and he went down with clutching fingers at his throat.

He doubled his knee and drove it hard into his assailant. 'Let me up or I'll kill you.'

Theremon cried out sharply and muttered through a blinding haze of pain. 'You double-crossing rat!'

The newsman seemed conscious of everything at once. He heard Beenay croak, 'I've got it. At your cameras, men!' and then there was the strange awareness that the last thread of sunlight had thinned out and snapped.

Simultaneously he heard one last choking gasp from Beenay, and a queer little cry from Sheerin, a hysterical giggle that cut off in a rasp – and a sudden silence, a strange, deadly silence from outside.

And Latimer had gone limp in his loosening grasp. Theremon peered into the Cultist's eyes and saw the blankness of them, staring upward, mirroring the feeble yellow of the torches. He saw the bubble of froth upon Latimer's lips and heard the low animal whimper in Latimer's throat.

With the slow fascination of fear, he lifted himself on one arm and turned his eyes toward the blood-curdling blackness of the window.

Through it shone the Stars!

Not Earth's feeble thirty-six hundred Stars visible to the eye; Lagash was in the center of a giant cluster. Thirty thousand mighty suns shone down in a soul-searing splendor that was more frighteningly cold in its awful indifference than the bitter wind that shivered across the cold, horribly bleak world.

Theremon staggered to his feet, his throat constricting him to breathlessness, all the muscles of his body writhing in an intensity of terror and sheer fear beyond bearing. He was going mad and knew it, and somewhere deep inside a bit of sanity was screaming, struggling to fight off the hopeless flood of black terror. It was very horrible to go mad and know that you were going mad – to know that in a little minute you would be here

physically and yet all the real essence would be dead and drowned
in the black madness. For this was the Dark – the Dark and the
Cold and the Doom. The bright walls of the universe were shattered and their awful black fragments were falling down to crush
and squeeze and obliterate him.

He jostled someone crawling on hands and knees, but stumbled somehow over him. Hands groping at his tortured throat,
he limped toward the flame of the torches that filled all his mad
vision.

'Light!' he screamed.

Aton, somewhere, was crying, whimpering horribly like a terribly frightened child. 'Stars – all the Stars – we didn't know at
all. We didn't know anything. We thought six stars in a universe
is something the Stars didn't notice is Darkness forever and ever
and ever and the walls are breaking in and we didn't know we
couldn't know and anything –'

Someone clawed at the torch, and it fell and snuffed out. In
the instant, the awful splendor of the indifferent Stars leaped
nearer to them.

On the horizon outside the window, in the direction of Saro
City, a crimson glow began growing, strengthening in bright-
ness, that was not the glow of a sun.

The long night had come again.

In 1948, I woke up one morning to read in the New York Times that Street & Smith Publications had discontinued all its pulp magazines.

Since Astounding Science Fiction was one of the Street & Smith pulps, everything went black before my eyes. You see, during the six-year period from 1943 to 1948 inclusive, I had sold and published thirteen science fiction stories, every single one of them to Astounding. During that period I had labored constantly with the feeling that I was not a writer at all, but merely a person who happened to click it off with one particular market, and that if anything happened to Astounding or to Mr. Campbell, its editor, I was through.

With great difficulty I finished the article and found, near the end, the utterly casual statement (almost as an afterthought) that Astounding was the one exception. It was the only pulp magazine Street & Smith was going to retain.

I was reprieved, but I still felt in a most fragile situation. Something might still happen to either Astounding or to Mr. Campbell. (Nothing did! At least so far! At this moment of writing, more than twenty years after that article, Astounding still flourishes, although it has a different publisher and has changed its name to Analog. And the durable Mr. Campbell is still its editor.)

I sold four more stories to Astounding in 1949 and 1950 before breaking the string. Then, in 1950, a new science fiction magazine came into sudden, vigorous life under the energetic leadership of its editor, Horace L. Gold.

Mr. Gold searched strenuously for stories while the new magazine was being formed and he asked me if I would submit some. I hesitated, for I was not at all sure that Mr. Gold would like them and I was wondering whether I could bear rejections that would serve as 'proof' that I was not a real writer but only a one-editor author.

Mr. Gold was, however, persuasive. I wrote two stories and he took them both. The first story, I felt, might have been a forced sale; he needed it for the maiden issue in a big hurry. The second story, which appeared in the second issue, did not have to be bought, it seemed to me. I accepted the sale as deserved and a more-than-seven-year agony of self-doubt was relieved. It is this second story which follows.

But one thing — editors have the frequent urge to change the *titles of stories. Heaven knows why! Some editors have it worse than others and Mr. Gold had a rather acute case.*

My own title for this story was 'Green Patches' for reasons that will seem perfectly clear when you read the story. For some obscure reason, Mr. Gold didn't like it and when the story appeared, it bore the name 'Misbegotten Missionary.' Except for the alliteration, I could see no reason why this new title should appeal to any rational person.

So I am seizing the opportunity now to change the title back to what it had been. I don't think I'm being hasty in doing so. I have been waiting eighteen years for a chance.

First appearance – Galaxy Science Fiction, *November 1950, under the title 'Misbegotten Missionary', Copyright, 1950, by World Editions, Inc.*

GREEN PATCHES

He had slipped aboard the ship! There had been dozens waiting outside the energy barrier when it had seemed that waiting would do no good. Then the barrier had faltered for a matter of two minutes (which showed the superiority of unified organisms over life fragments) and he was across.

None of the others had been able to move quickly enough to take advantage of the break, but that didn't matter. All alone, he was enough. No others were necessary.

And the thought faded out of satisfaction and into loneliness. It was a terribly unhappy and unnatural thing to be parted from all the rest of the unified organism, to be a life fragment oneself. How could these aliens stand being fragments?

It increased his sympathy for the aliens. Now that he experienced fragmentation himself, he could feel, as though from a distance, the terrible isolation that made them so afraid. It was fear born of that isolation that dictated their actions. What but the insane fear of their condition could have caused them to blast an area, one mile in diameter, into dull-red heat before landing their ship? Even the organized life ten feet deep in the soil had been destroyed in the blast.

He engaged reception, listening eagerly, letting the alien thoughts saturate him. He enjoyed the touch of life upon his consciousness. He would have to ration that enjoyment. He must not forget himself.

But it could do no harm to listen to thoughts. Some of the fragments of life on the ship thought quite clearly, considering that they were such primitive, incomplete creatures. Their thoughts were like tiny bells.

Roger Oldenn said, 'I feel contaminated. You know what I mean? I keep washing my hands and it doesn't help.'

Jerry Thorn hated dramatics and didn't look up. They were still maneuvering in the stratosphere of Saybrook's Planet and he preferred to watch the panel dials. He said, 'No reason to feel contaminated. Nothing happened.'

'I hope not,' said Oldenn. 'At least they had all the field men discard their spacesuits in the air lock for complete disinfection. They had a radiation bath for all men entering from outside. I *suppose* nothing happened.'

'Why be nervous, then?'

'I don't know. I wish the barrier hadn't broken down.'

'Who doesn't? It was an accident.'

'I wonder.' Oldenn was vehement. 'I was here when it happened. My shift, you know. There was no reason to overload the power line. There was equipment plugged into it that had no damn business near it. None whatsoever.'

'All right. People are stupid.'

'Not that stupid. I hung around when the Old Man was checking into the matter. None of them had reasonable excuses. The armor-baking circuits, which were draining off two thousand watts, had been put into the barrier line. They'd been using the second subsidiaries for a week. Why not this time? They couldn't give any reason.'

'Can you?'

Oldenn flushed. 'No, I was just wondering if the men had been' – he searched for a word – 'hypnotized into it. By those things outside.'

Thorn's eyes lifted and met those of the other levelly. 'I

wouldn't repeat that to anyone else. The barrier was down only two minutes. If anything had happened, if even a spear of grass had drifted across it would have shown up in our bacteria cultures within half an hour, in the fruit-fly colonies in a matter of days. Before we got back it would show up in the hamsters, the rabbits, maybe the goats. Just get it through your head, Oldenn, that nothing happened. Nothing.'

Oldenn turned on his heel and left. In leaving, his foot came within two feet of the object in the corner of the room. He did not see it.

He disengaged his reception centers and let the thoughts flow past him unperceived. These life fragments were not important, in any case, since they were not fitted for the continuation of life. Even as fragments, they were incomplete.

The other types of fragments now – they were different. He had to be careful of them. The temptation would be great, and he must give no indication, none at all, of his existence on board ship till they landed on their home planet.

He focused on the other parts of the ship, marveling at the diversity of life. Each item, no matter how small, was sufficient to itself. He forced himself to contemplate this, until the unpleasantness of the thought grated on him and he longed for the normality of home.

Most of the thoughts he received from the smaller fragments were vague and fleeting, as you would expect. There wasn't much to be had from them, but that meant their need for completeness was all the greater. It was that which touched him so keenly.

There was the life fragment which squatted on its haunches and fingered the wire netting that enclosed it. Its thoughts were clear, but limited. Chiefly, they concerned the yellow fruit a companion fragment was eating. It wanted the fruit very deeply. Only the wire netting that separated the fragments prevented its seizing the fruit by force.

He disengaged reception in a moment of complete revulsion. *These fragments competed for food!*

He tried to reach far outward for the peace and harmony of home, but it was already an immense distance away. He could reach only into the nothingness that separated him from sanity.

He longed at the moment even for the feel of the dead soil between the barrier and the ship. He had crawled over it last

night. There had been no life upon it, but it had been the soil of
home, and on the other side of the barrier there had still been the
comforting feel of the rest of organized life.

He could remember the moment he had located himself on
the surface of the ship, maintaining a desperate suction grip
until the air lock opened. He had entered, moving cautiously
between the outgoing feet. There had been an inner lock and
that had been passed later. Now he lay here, a life fragment himself, inert and unnoticed.

Cautiously, he engaged reception again at the previous focus.
The squatting fragment of life was tugging furiously at the wire
netting. It still wanted the other's food, though it was the less
hungry of the two.

Larsen said, 'Don't feed the damn thing. She isn't hungry;
she's just sore because Tillie had the nerve to eat before she herself was crammed full. The greedy ape! I wish we were back
home and I never had to look another animal in the face again.'

He scowled at the older female chimpanzee frowningly and
the chimp mouthed and chattered back to him in full reciproca-
tion.

Rizzo said, 'Okay, okay. Why hang around here, then? Feed-
ing time is over. Let's get out.'

They went past the goat pens, the rabbit hutches, the hamster
cages.

Larsen said bitterly, 'You volunteer for an exploration voy-
age. You're a hero. They send you off with speeches – and make
a zoo keeper out of you.'

'They give you double pay.'

'All right, so what? I didn't sign up just for the money. They
said at the original briefing that it was even odds we wouldn't
come back, that we'd end up like Saybrook. I signed up because
I wanted to do something important.'

'Just a bloomin' bloody hero,' said Rizzo.

'I'm not an animal nurse.'

Rizzo paused to lift a hamster out of the cage and stroke it.
'Hey,' he said, 'did you ever think that maybe one of these hamsters has some cute little baby hamsters inside, just getting started?'

'Wise guy! They're tested every day.'

'Sure, sure.' He muzzled the little creature, which vibrated its nose at him. 'But just suppose you came down one morning and found them there. New little hamsters looking up at you with soft, green patches of fur where the eyes ought to be.'

'Shut up, for the love of Mike,' yelled Larsen.

'Little soft, green patches of shining fur,' said Rizzo, and put the hamster down with a sudden loathing sensation.

He engaged reception again and varied the focus. There wasn't a specialized life fragment at home that didn't have a rough counterpart on shipboard.

There were the moving runners in various shapes, the moving swimmers, and the moving flyers. Some of the flyers were quite large, with perceptible thoughts; others were small, gauzy-winged creatures. These last transmitted only patterns of sense perception, imperfect patterns at that, and added nothing intelligent of their own.

There were the non-movers, which, like the non-movers at home, were green and lived on the air, water, and soil. These were a mental blank. They knew only the dim, dim consciousness of light, moisture, and gravity.

And each fragment, moving and non-moving, had its mockery of life.

Not yet. Not yet. . . .

He clamped down hard upon his feelings. Once before, these life fragments had come, and the rest at home had tried to help them – too quickly. It had not worked. This time they must wait.

If only these fragments did not discover him.

They had not, so far. They had not noticed him lying in the corner of the pilot room. No one had bent down to pick up and discard him. Earlier, it had meant he could not move. Someone might have turned and stared at the stiff wormlike thing, not quite six inches long. First stare, then shout, and then it would all be over.

But now, perhaps, he had waited long enough. The take-off was long past. The controls were locked; the pilot room was empty.

It did not take him long to find the chink in the armor leading to the recess where some of the wiring was. They were dead wires.

The front end of his body was a rasp that cut in two a wire of just the right diameter. Then, six inches away, he cut it in two again. He pushed the snipped-off section of the wire ahead of him packing it away neatly and invisibly into a corner of the recess. Its outer covering was a brown elastic material and its core was gleaming, ruddy metal. He himself could not reproduce the core, of course, but that was not necessary. It was enough that the pellicle that covered him had been carefully bred to resemble a wire's surface.

He returned and grasped the cut section of the wire before and behind. He tightened against them as his little suction disks came into play. Not even a seam showed.

They could not find him now. They could look right at him and see only a continuous stretch of wire.

Unless they looked very closely indeed and noted that, in a certain spot on this wire, there were two tiny patches of soft and shining green fur.

'It is remarkable,' said Dr. Weiss, 'that little green hairs can do so much.'

Captain Loring poured the brandy carefully. In a sense, this was a celebration. They would be ready for the jump through hyper-space in two hours, and after that, two days would see them back on Earth.

'You are convinced, then, the green fur is the sense organ?' he asked.

'It is,' said Weiss. Brandy made him come out in splotches, but he was aware of the need of celebration – quite aware. 'The experiments were conducted under difficulties, but they were quite significant.'

The captain smiled stiffly. ' "Under difficulties" is one way of phrasing it. I would never have taken the chances you did to run them.'

'Nonsense. We're all heroes aboard this ship, all volunteers, all great men with trumpet, fife, and fanfaronade. You took the chance of coming here.'

'You were the first to go outside the barrier.'

'No particular risk was involved,' Weiss said. 'I burned the ground before me as I went, to say nothing of the portable barrier that surrounded me. Nonsense, Captain. Let's all take our medals when we come back; let's take them without attempt at gradation. Besides, I'm a male.'

'But you're filled with bacteria to here.' The captain's hand made a quick, cutting gesture three inches above his head. 'which makes you as vulnerable as a female would be.'

They paused for drinking purposes.

'Refill?' asked the captain.

'No, thanks. I've exceeded my quota already.'

'Then one last for the spaceroad.' He lifted his glass in the general direction of Saybrook's Planet, no longer visible, its sun only a bright star in the visiplate. 'To the little green hairs that gave Saybrook his first lead.'

Weiss nodded. 'A lucky thing. We'll quarantine the planet, of course.'

The captain said, 'That doesn't seem drastic enough. Someone might always land by accident someday and not have Saybrook's insight, or his guts. Suppose he did not blow up his ship, as Saybrook did. Suppose he got back to some inhabited place.'

The captain was somber. 'Do you suppose they might ever develop interstellar travel on their own?'

'I doubt it. No proof, of course. It's just that they have such a completely different orientation. Their entire organization of life has made tools unnecessary. As far as we know, even a stone ax doesn't exist on the planet.'

'I hope you're right. Oh, and, Weiss, would you spend some time with Drake?'

'The Galactic Press fellow?'

'Yes. Once we get back, the story of Saybrook's Planet will be released for the public and I don't think it would be wise to over-sensationalize it. I've asked Drake to let you consult with him on the story. You're a biologist and enough of an authority to carry weight with him. Would you oblige?'

'A pleasure.'

The captain closed his eyes wearily and shook his head.

'Headache, Captain?'

'No. Just thinking of poor Saybrook.'

He was weary of the ship. A while back there had been a queer, momentary sensation, as though he had been turned inside out. It was alarming and he had searched the minds of the keen-thinkers for an explanation. Apparently the ship had leaped across vast stretches of empty space by cutting across something they knew as 'hyper-space'. The keen-thinkers were ingenious.

But – he was weary of the ship. It was such a futile phenomenon. These life fragments were skilful in their constructions, yet it was only a measure of their unhappiness, after all. They strove to find in the control of inanimate matter what they could not find in themselves. In their unconscious yearning for completeness, they built machines and scoured space, seeking, seeking . . .

These creatures, he knew, could never, in the very nature of things, find that for which they were seeking. At least not until such time as he gave it to them. He quivered a little at the thought.

Completeness!

These fragments had no concept of it, even. 'Completeness' was a poor word.

In their ignorance they would even fight it. There had been the ship that had come before. The first ship had contained many of the keen-thinking fragments. There had been two varieties, life producers and the sterile ones. (How different this second ship was. The keen-thinkers were all sterile, while the other fragments, the fuzzy-thinkers and the no-thinkers, were all producers of life. It was strange.)

How gladly that first ship had been welcomed by all the planet! He could remember the first intense shock at the realization that the visitors were fragments and not complete. The shock had given way to pity, and the pity to action. It was not certain how they would fit into the community, but there had been no hesitation. All life was sacred and somehow room would have been made for them – for all of them, from the large keen-thinkers to the little multipliers in the darkness.

But there had been a miscalculation. They had not correctly analyzed the course of the fragments' ways of thinking. The keen-thinkers became aware of what had been done and resented it. They were frightened, of course; they did not understand.

They had developed the barrier first, and then, later, had destroyed themselves, exploding their ship to atoms.

Poor, foolish fragments.

This time, at least, it would be different. They would be saved, despite themselves.

John Drake would not have admitted it in so many words, but he was very proud of his skill on the photo-typer. He had

a travel-kit model, which was a six-by-eight, featureless dark
plastic slab, with cylindrical bulges on either end to hold the
roll of thin paper. It fitted into a brown leather case, equipped
with a beltlike contraption that held it closely about the waist
and at one hip. The whole thing weighed less than a pound.

Drake could operate it with either hand. His fingers would
flick quickly and easily, placing their light pressure at exact spots
on the blank surface, and, soundlessly, words would be written.

He looked thoughtfully at the beginning of his story, then up
at Dr. Weiss. 'What do you think, Doc?'

'It starts well.'

Drake nodded. 'I thought I might as well start with Saybrook
himself. They haven't released his story back home yet. I wish
I could have seen Saybrook's original report. How did he ever get
it through, by the way?'

'As near as I could could tell, he spent one last night sending it
through the sub-ether. When he was finished, he shorted the
motors, and converted the entire ship into a thin cloud of vapor
a millionth of a second later. The crew and himself along with
it.'

'What a man! You were in this from the beginning, Doc?'

'Not from the beginning,' corrected Weiss gently. 'Only since
the receipt of Saybrook's report.'

He could not help thinking back. He had read that report,
realizing even then how wonderful the planet must have seemed
when Saybrook's colonizing expedition first reached it. It was
practically a duplicate of Earth, with an abounding plant life
and a purely vegetarian animal life.

There had been only the little patches of green fur (how often
had he used that phrase in his speaking and thinking!) which
seemed strange. No living individual on the planet had eyes.
Instead, there was this fur. Even the plants, each blade or leaf
or blossom, possessed the two patches of richer green.

Then Saybrook had noticed, startled and bewildered, that
there was no conflict for food on the planet. All plants grew
pulpy appendages which were eaten by the animals. These were
regrown in a matter of hours. No other parts of the plants were
touched. It was as though the plants fed the animals as part of
the order of nature. And the plants themselves did not grow in
overpowering profusion. They might almost have been culti-
vated, they were spread across the available soil so discriminately.

How much time, Weiss wondered, had Saybrook had to observe the strange law and order on the planet? – the fact that insects kept their numbers reasonable, though no birds ate them; that the rodent-like things did not swarm, though no carnivores existed to keep them in check.

And then there had come the incident of the white rats.

That prodded Weiss. He said, 'Oh, one correction, Drake. Hamsters were not the first animals involved. It was the white rats.'

'White rats,' said Drake, making the correction in his notes.

'Every colonizing ship,' said Weiss, 'takes a group of white rats for the purpose of testing any alien foods. Rats, of course, are very similar to human beings from a nutritional viewpoint. Naturally, only female white rats are taken.'

Naturally. If only one sex were present, there was no danger of unchecked multiplication in case the planet proved favorable. Remember the rabbits in Australia.

'Incidentally, why not use males?' asked Drake.

'Females are hardier,' said Weiss, 'which is lucky, since that gave the situation away. It turned out suddenly that all the rats were bearing young.'

'Right. Now that's where I'm up to, so here's my chance to get some things straight. For my own information, Doc, how did Saybrook find out they were in the family way?'

'Accidentally, of course. In the course of nutritional investigations, rats are dissected for evidence of internal damage. Their condition was bound to be discovered. A few more were dissected; same results. Eventually, all that lived gave birth to young – with *no* male rats aboard!'

'And the point is that all the young were born with little green patches of fur instead of eyes.'

'That is correct. Saybrook said so and we corroborate him. After the rats, the pet cat of one of the children was obviously affected. When it finally kittened, the kittens were not born with closed eyes but with little patches of green fur. There was no tomcat aboard.

'Eventually Saybrook had the women tested. He didn't tell them what for. He didn't want to frighten them. Every single one of them was in the early stages of pregnancy, leaving out of consideration those few who had been pregnant at the time of embarkation. Saybrook never waited for any child to be born, of course. He knew they would have no eyes, only shining patches of green fur.

'He even prepared bacterial cultures (Saybrook was a thorough man) and found each bacillus to show microscopic green spots.'

Drake was eager. 'That goes way beyond our briefing – or, at least, the briefing I got. But granted that life on Saybrook's Planet is organized into a unified whole, how is it done?'

'How? How are your cells organized into a unified whole? Take an individual cell out of your body, even a brain cell, and what is it by itself? Nothing. A little blob of protoplasm with no more capacity for anything human than an amoeba. Less capacity, in fact, since it couldn't live by itself. But put the cells together and you have something that could invent a spaceship or write a symphony.'

'I get the idea,' said Drake.

Weiss went on, '*All* life on Saybrook's Planet is a *single* organism. In a sense, all life on Earth is too, but it's a fighting dependence, a dog-eat-dog dependence. The bacteria fix nitrogen; the plants fix carbon; animals eat plants and each other; bacterial decay hits everything. It comes full circle. Each grabs as much as it can, and is, in turn, grabbed.

'On Saybrook's Planet, each organism has its place, as each cell in our body does. Bacteria and plants produce food, on the excess of which animals feed, providing in turn carbon dioxide and nitrogenous wastes. Nothing is produced more or less than is needed. The scheme of life is intelligently altered to suit the local environment. No group of life forms multiplies more or less than is needed, just as the cells in our body stop multiplying when there are enough of them for a given purpose. When they don't stop multiplying, we call it cancer. And that's what life on Earth really is, the kind of organic organization we have, compared to that on Saybrook's Planet. One big cancer. Every species, every individual doing its best to thrive at the expense of every other species and individual.'

'You sound as if you approve of Saybrook's Planet, Doc.'

'I do, in a way. It makes sense out of the business of living. I can see their viewpoint toward us. Suppose one of the cells of your body could be conscious of the efficiency of the human body as compared with that of the cell itself, and could realize that this was only the result of the union of many cells into a higher whole. And then suppose it became conscious of the existence of free-living cells, with bare life and nothing more. It might feel a very strong desire to drag the poor thing into an organization. It might feel sorry for it, feel perhaps a sort of missionary spirit. The things on Saybrook's Planet — or the thing; one should use the singular — feels just that, perhaps.'

'And went ahead by bringing about virgin births, eh, Doc? I've got to go easy on that angle of it. Post-office regulations, you know.'

'There's nothing ribald about it, Drake. For centuries we've been able to make the eggs of sea urchins, bees, frogs, et cetera develop without the intervention of male fertilization. The touch of a needle was sometimes enough, or just immersion in the proper salt solution. The thing on Saybrook's Planet can cause fertilization by the controlled use of radiant energy. That's why an appropriate energy barrier stops it; interference, you see, or static.

'They can do more than stimulate the division and development of an unfertilized egg. They can impress their own characteristics upon its nucleoproteins, so that the young are born with the little patches of green fur, which serve as the planet's sense organ and means of communication. The young, in other words, are not individuals, but become part of the thing on Saybrook's Planet. The thing on the planet, not at all incidentally, can impregnate any species — plant, animal, or microscopic.'

'Potent stuff,' muttered Drake.

'Totipotent,' Dr. Weiss said sharply. 'Universally potent. Any fragment of it is totipotent. Given time, a single bacterium from Saybrook's Planet can convert *all of Earth* into a single organism! We've got the experimental proof of that.'

Drake said unexpectedly, 'You know, I think I'm a millionaire, Doc. Can you keep a secret?'

Weiss nodded, puzzled.

'I've got a souvenir from Saybrook's Planet,' Drake told him, grinning. 'It's only a pebble, but after the publicity the planet will get, combined with the fact that it's quarantined from here on in, the pebble will be all any human being will ever see of it. How much do you suppose I could sell the thing for?'

Weiss stared. 'A pebble?' He snatched at the object shown him, a hard, gray ovoid. 'You shouldn't have done that, Drake. It was strictly against regulations.'

'I know. That's why I asked if you could keep a secret. If you could give me a signed note of authentication – *What's the matter, Doc?*'

Instead of answering, Weiss could only chatter and point. Drake ran over and stared down at the pebble. It was the same as before –

Except that the light was catching it at an angle, and it showed up two little green spots. Look very closely; they were patches of green hairs.

He was disturbed. There was a definite air of danger within the ship. There was the suspicion of his presence aboard. How could that be? He had done nothing yet. Had another fragment of home come aboard and been less cautious? That would be impossible without his knowledge, and though he probed the ship intensely, he found nothing.

And then the suspicion diminished, but it was not quite dead. One of the keen-thinkers still wondered, and was treading close to the truth.

How long before the landing? Would an entire world of life fragments be deprived of completeness? He clung closer to the severed ends of the wire he had been specially bred to imitate, afraid of detection, fearful for his altruistic mission.

Dr. Weiss had locked himself in his own room. They were already within the solar system, and in three hours they would be landing. He had to think. He had three hours in which to decide.

Drake's devilish 'pebble' had been part of the organized life on Saybrook's Planet, of course, but it was dead. It was dead when he had first seen it, and if it hadn't been, it was certainly dead after they fed it into the hyper-atomic motor and converted it into a blast of pure heat. And the bacterial cultures still showed normal when Weiss anxiously checked.

That was not what bothered Weiss now.

Drake had picked up the 'pebble' during the last hours of the stay on Saybrook's Planet – *after* the barrier breakdown. What if the breakdown had been the result of a slow, relentless mental pressure on the part of the thing on the planet? What if parts of its being waited to invade as the barrier dropped? If the 'pebble' had not been fast enough and had moved only after the barrier was re-established, it would have been killed. It would have lain there for Drake to see and pick up.

It was a 'pebble,' not a natural life form. But did that mean it was not *some* kind of life form? It might have been a deliberate production of the planet's single organism – a creature deliberately designed to look like a pebble, harmless-seeming, unsuspicious. Camouflage, in other words – a shrewd and frighteningly successful camouflage.

Had any other camouflaged creature succeeded in crossing the barrier *before* it was re-established – with a suitable shape filched from the minds of the humans aboard ship by the mind-reading organism of the planet? Would it have the casual appearance of a paperweight? Of an ornamental brass-head nail in the captain's old-fashioned chair? And how would they locate it? Could they search every part of the ship for the telltale green patches – even down to individual microbes?

And why camouflage? Did it intend to remain undetected for a time? Why? So that it might wait for the landing on Earth?

An infection *after landing* could not be cured by blowing up a ship. The bacteria of Earth, the molds, yeasts, and protozoa, would go first. Within a year the non-human young would begin arriving by the uncountable billions.

Weiss closed his eyes and told himself it might not be such a bad thing. There would be no more disease, since no bacterium would multiply at the expense of its host, but instead would be satisfied with its fair share of what was available. There would be no more overpopulation; the hordes of mankind would decline to adjust themselves to the food supply. There would be no more wars, no crime, no greed.

But there would be no more individuality, either.

Humanity would find security by becoming a cog in a biological machine. A man would be brother to a germ, or to a liver cell.

He stood up. He would have a talk with Captain Loring. They would send their report and blow up the ship, just as Saybrook had done.

He sat down again. Saybrook had had proof, while he had only the conjectures of a terrorized mind, rattled by the sight of two green spots on a pebble. Could he kill the two hundred men on board ship because of a feeble suspicion?

He had to *think!*

He was shivering. Why did he have to wait? If he could only welcome those who were aboard now. *Now!*

Yet a cooler, more reasoning part of himself told him that he could not. The little multipliers in the darkness would betray their new status in fifteen minutes, and the keen-thinkers had them under continual observation. Even one mile from the surface of their planet would be too soon, since they might still destroy themselves and their ship out in space.

Better to wait for the main air locks to open, for the planetary air to swirl in with millions of the little multipliers. Better to greet each one of them into the brotherhood of unified life and let them swirl out again to spread the message.

Then it would be done! Another world organized, complete!

He waited. There was the dull throbbing of the engines working mightily to control the slow dropping of the ship; the shudder of contact with planetary surface, then –

He let the jubilation of the keen-thinkers sweep into reception, and his own jubilant thoughts answered them. Soon they would be able to receive as well as himself. Perhaps not these particular fragments, but the fragments that would grow out of those which were fitted for the continuation of life.

The main air locks were about to be opened –

And all thought ceased.

Jerry Thorn thought, Damn it, something's wrong *now*.

He said to Captain Loring, 'Sorry. There seems to be a power breakdown. The locks won't open.'

'Are you sure, Thorn? The lights are on.'

'Yes, sir. We're investigating it now.'

He tore away and joined Roger Oldenn at the air-lock wiring box. 'What's wrong?'

'Give me a chance, will you?' Oldenn's hands were busy. Then he said, 'For the love of Pete, there's a six-inch break in the twenty-amp lead.'

'What? That can't be!'

Oldenn held up the broken wires with their clean, sharp, sawn-through ends.

Dr. Weiss joined them. He looked haggard and there was the smell of brandy on his breath.

He said shakily, 'What's the matter?'

They told him. At the bottom of the compartment, in one

corner, was the missing section.

Weiss bent over. There was a black fragment on the floor of the compartment. He touched it with his finger and it smeared, leaving a sooty smudge on his finger-tip. He rubbed it off absently.

There might have been something taking the place of the missing section of wire. Something that had been alive and only looked like wire, yet something that would heat, die, and carbonize in a tiny fraction of a second once the electrical circuit which controlled the air lock had been closed.

He said, 'How are the bacteria?'

A crew member went to check, returned and said, 'All normal, Doc.'

The wires had meanwhile been spliced, the locks opened, and Dr. Weiss stepped out into the anarchic world of life that was Earth.

'Anarchy,' he said, laughing a little wildly. 'And it will stay that way.'

By late 1950, my wife and I had come to the sad and reluctant conclusion that we were not going to have any children. There was nothing particularly wrong that anyone could find, but neither was anything happening.

My wife therefore decided we might as well adjust our way of life to childlessness and prepared to take a greater role in my continuing-to-expand writing career. It seemed to us that efficiency might be increased if we worked as a team. I would dictate my stories and she would type them.

I was a little dubious. It sounded great in theory, but I had never dictated a story. I was used to typing my stories and watching the sentences appear steadily, word by word. So I did not buy a dictating machine outright. I talked the salesman into letting me have it on thirty-day approval.

In the course of the next month, I dictated three stories into the machine, of which 'Hostess' was one. It was a frightening experience that taught me a few things. For instance, I discovered that I participated in a story to a greater extent than I realized, when my wife came to me with a little plastic record and said 'I can't type this.'

I listened to the passage she objected to, one in which two of my characters were quarrelling with greater and greater vehemence. I found that as they grew more emotional, so did I, and when their quarrel reached its peak, I was making nothing more than incoherent sounds of rage. I had to dictate that part over again. Heavens, it never happens when I type.

But it worked out well. When the stories were typed up, they sounded just like me; just as though I had typed them from the start. (At least so it seemed to me. You can read 'Hostess' and judge for yourself.)

Naturally, I was delighted. I looked up the salesman and told him I would buy the machine. I made out a check for the entire payment in a lump sum.

Within a week, however, according to later calculations, we managed to get a child started. When the fact became unmistakable, we had a conversation in which my contribution consisted entirely of a frequently interjected 'You're kidding!'

Anyway, the dictating machine was never used again, though we still own it. Four months after 'Hostess' appeared, my son, David, was born.

First appearance – Galaxy Science Fiction, *May 1951. Copyright, 1951, by World Editions, Inc.*

HOSTESS

Rose Smollet was happy about it; almost triumphant. She peeled off her gloves, put her hat away, and turned her brightening eyes upon her husband.

She said, 'Drake, we're going to have him here.'

Drake looked at her with annoyance. 'You've missed supper. I thought you were going to be back by seven'.

'Oh, that doesn't matter. I ate something on the way home. But, Drake, we're going to have him here!'

'*Who* here? What are you talking about?'

'The doctor from Hawkin's Planet! Didn't you realize that was what today's conference was about? We spent all day talking about it. It's the most exciting thing that could possibly have happened!'

Drake Smollett removed the pipe from the vicinity of his face. He stared first at it and then at his wife. 'Let me get this straight. When you say the doctor from Hawkin's Planet, do you mean the Hawkinsite you've got at the Institute?'

'Well, of course. Who else could I possibly mean?'

'And may I ask what the devil you mean by saying we'll have him here?'

'Drake, don't you understand?'

'What is there to understand? Your Institute may be interested in the thing, but I'm not. What have we to do with it personally? It's Institute business, isn't it?'

'But, darling,' Rose said, patiently, 'the Hawkinsite would like to stay at a private house somewhere, where he won't be bothered with official ceremony, and where he'll be able to proceed more according to his own likes and dislikes. I find it quite understandable.'

'Why at *our* house?'

'Because our place is convenient for the purpose, I suppose. They asked if I would allow it, and frankly,' she added with some stiffness, 'I consider it a privilege.'

'Look!' Drake put his fingers through his brown hair and succeeded in rumpling it. 'We've got a convenient little place here – granted! It's not the most elegant place in the world, but it does well enough for us. However, I don't see where we've got room for extraterrestrial visitors.'

Rose began to look worried. She removed her glasses and put them away in their case. 'He can stay in the spare room. He'll take care of it himself. I've spoken to him and he's very pleasant. Honestly, all we have to do is show a certain amount of adaptability.'

Drake said, 'Sure, just a little adaptability! The Hawkinsites breathe cyanide. We'll just adapt ourselves to that, I suppose!'

'He carries cyanide in a little cylinder. You won't even notice it.'

'And what else about them that I won't notice?'

'*Nothing* else. They're perfectly harmless. Goodness, they're even vegetarians.'

'And what does that mean? Do we feed him a bale of hay for dinner?'

Rose's lower lip trembled. 'Drake, you're being deliberately hateful. There are many vegetarians on Earth; they don't eat hay.'

'And what about us? Do we eat meat ourselves or will that make us look like cannibals to him? I won't live on salads to suit him; I warn you.'

'You're being quite ridiculous.'

Rose felt helpless. She had married late in life, comparatively. Her career had been chosen; she herself had seemed well settled in it. She was a fellow in biology at the Jenkins Institute for the Natural Sciences, with over twenty publications to her credit. In a word, the line was hewed, the path cleared; she had been set for a career and spinsterhood. And now, at 35, she was still a little amazed to find herself a bride of less than a year.

Occasionally, it embarrassed her, too, since she sometimes found that she had not the slightest idea of how to handle her husband. What *did* one do when the man of the family became mulish? That was not included in any of her courses. As a woman of independent mind and career, she couldn't bring herself to cajolery.

So she looked at him steadily and said simply, 'It means very much to me.'

'Why?'

'Because, Drake, if he stays here for any length of time, I can study him really closely. Very little work has been done on the biology and psychology of the individual Hawkinsite or of any of the extraterrestrial intelligences. We have some of their sociology and history, of course, but that's all. Surely, you must see the opportunity. He stays here; we watch him, speak to him, observe his habits –'

'Not interested.'

'Oh, Drake, I don't understand you.'

'You're going to say I'm not usually like this, I suppose.'

'Well, you're not.'

Drake was silent for a while. He seemed withdrawn and his high cheekbones and large chin were twisted and frozen into a brooding position.

He said finally, 'Look, I've heard a bit about the Hawkinsites in the way of my own business. You say there have been investigations of their sociology, but not of their biology. Sure. It's because the Hawkinsites don't like to be studied as specimens any more than we would. I've spoken to men who were in charge of security groups watching various Hawkinsite missions on Earth. The missions stay in the rooms assigned to them and don't leave for anything but the most important official business. They have nothing to do with Earthmen. It's quite obvious that they are as revolted by us as I personally am by them.

'In fact, I just don't understand why this Hawkinsite at the Institute should be any different. It seems to me to be against all the rules to have him come here by himself, anyway – and to have him want to stay in an Earthman's home just puts the maraschino cherry on top.'

Rose said, wearily, 'This is different. I'm surprised you can't understand it, Drake. He's a doctor. He's coming here in the way of medical research, and I'll grant you that he probably doesn't enjoy staying with human beings and will find us perfectly horrible. But he must stay just the same! Do you suppose human doctors enjoy going into the tropics, or that they are particularly fond of letting themselves be bitten by infected mosquitoes?'

Drake said sharply, 'What's this about mosquitoes? What have they to do with it?'

'Why, nothing,' Rose answered, surprised. 'It just came to my mind, that's all. I was thinking of Reed and his yellow-fever experiments.'

Drake shrugged. 'Well, have it your own way.'

For a moment, Rose hesitated. 'You're not angry about this, are you?' To her own ears she sounded unpleasantly girlish.

'No.'

And that, Rose knew, meant that he was.

Rose surveyed herself doubtfully in the full-length mirror. She had never been beautiful and was quite reconciled to the fact; so much so that it no longer mattered. Certainly, it would not matter to a being from Hawkin's Planet. What *did* bother her was this matter of being a hostess under the very queer circumstances of having to be tactful to an extraterrestrial creature and, at the same time, to her husband as well. She wondered which would prove the more difficult.

Drake was coming home late that day; he was not due for half an hour. Rose found herself inclined to believe that he had arranged that purposely in a sullen desire to leave her alone with her problem. She found herself in a state of mild resentment.

He had called her just before noon at the Institute and had asked abruptly, 'When are you taking him home?'

She answered, curtly, 'In about three hours.'

'All right. What's his name? His Hawkinsite name?'

'Why do you want to know?' She could not keep the chill from her words.

'Let's call it a small investigation of my own. After all, the thing will be in my house.'

'Oh, for heaven's sake, Drake, don't bring your job home with you!'

Drake's voice sounded tinny and nasty in her ears. 'Why not, Rose? Isn't that exactly what you're doing?'

It was, of course, so she gave him the information he wanted.

This was the first time in their married life that they had had even the semblance of a quarrel, and, as she sat there before the full-length mirror, she began to wonder if perhaps she ought not to make an attempt to see his side of it. In essence, she had mar-

ried a policeman. Of course he was more than simply a policeman; he was a member of the World Security Board.

It had been a surprise to her friends. The fact of the marriage
itself had been the biggest surprise, but if she had decided on
marriage, the attitude was, why not with another biologist? Or,
if she had wanted to go further afield, an anthropologist, perhaps;
even a chemist; but why, of all people, a policeman? Nobody had
exactly said those things, naturally, but it had been in the very
atmosphere at the time of her marriage.

She had resented it then, and ever since. A man could marry
whom he chose, but if a doctor of philosophy, female variety,
chose to marry a man who never went past the bachelor's degree,
there was shock. Why should there be? What business was it of
theirs? He was handsome, in a way, intelligent, in another way,
and she was perfectly satisfied with her choice.

Yet how much of this same snobbishness did she bring home
with her? Didn't she always have the attitude that her own
work, her biological investigations, were important, while his job
was merely something to be kept within the four walls of his
little office in the old U.N. buildings on the East River?

She jumped up from her seat in agitation and, with a deep
breath, decided to leave such thoughts behind her. She desperately did not want to quarrel with him. And she just wasn't going
to interfere with him. She was committed to accepting the Hawkinsite as guest, but otherwise she would let Drake have his own
way. He was making enough of a concession as it was.

Harg Tholan was standing quietly in the middle of the living
room when she came down the stairs. He was not sitting, since
he was not anatomically constructed to sit. He stood on two sets
of limbs placed close together, while a third pair entirely different in construction were suspended from a region that would
have been the upper chest in a human being. The skin of his
body was hard, glistening and ridged, while his face bore a distant resemblance to something alienly bovine. Yet he was not
completely repulsive, and he wore clothes of a sort over the lower
portion of his body in order to avoid offending the sensibilities
of his human hosts.

He said, 'Mrs. Smollett, I appreciate your hospitality beyond
my ability to express it in your language,' and he drooped so that
his forelimbs touched the ground for a moment.

Rose knew this to be a gesture signifying gratitude among the beings of Hawkin's Planet. She was grateful that he spoke English as well as he did. The construction of his mouth, combined with an absence of incisors, gave a whistling sound to the sibilants. Aside from that, he might have been born on Earth for all the accent his speech showed.

She said, 'My husband will be home soon, and then we will eat.'

'Your husband?' For a moment, he said nothing more, and then added, 'Yes, of course.'

She let it go. If there was one source of infinite confusion among the five intelligent races of the known Galaxy, it lay in the differences among them with regard to their sex life and the social institutions that grew around it. The concept of husband and wife, for instance, existed only on Earth. The other races could achieve a sort of intellectual understanding of what it meant, but never an emotional one.

She said, 'I have consulted the Institute in preparing your menu. I trust you will find nothing in it that will upset you.'

The Hawkinsite blinked its eyes rapidly. Rose recalled this to be a gesture of amusement.

He said, 'Proteins are proteins, my dear Mrs. Smollett. For those trace factors which I need but are not supplied in your food, I have brought concentrates that will be most adequate.'

And proteins *were* proteins. Rose knew this to be true. Her concern for the creature's diet had been largely one of formal politeness. In the discovery of life on the planets of the outer stars, one of the most interesting generalizations that had developed was the fact that, although life could be formed on the basis of substances other than proteins – even on elements other than carbon – it remained true that the only known intelligences were proteinaceous in nature. This meant that each of the five forms of intelligent life could maintain themselves over prolonged periods on the food of any of the other four.

She heard Drake's key in the door and went stiff with apprehension.

She had to admit he did well. He strode in, and without hesitation, thrust his hand out at the Hawkinsite, saying firmly, 'Good evening, Dr. Tholan.'

The Hawkinsite put out his large and rather clumsy forelimb

and the two, so to speak, shook hands. Rose had already gone through that procedure and knew the queer feeling of a Hawkinsite hand in her own. It had felt rough and hot and dry. She imagined that, to the Hawkinsite, her own and Drake's felt cold and slimy.

At the time of the formal greeting, she had taken the opportunity to observe the alien hand. It was an excellent case of converging evolution. Its morphological development was entirely different from that of the human hand, yet it had brought itself into a fairly approximate similarity. There were four fingers but no thumb. Each finger had five independent ball-and-socket joints. In this way, the flexibility lost with the absence of the thumb was made up for by the almost tentacular properties of the fingers. What was even more interesting to her biologist's eyes was the fact that each Hawkinsite finger ended in a vestigial hoof, very small and, to the layman, unidentifiable as such, but clearly adapted at one time to running, just as man's had been to climbing.

Drake said, in friendly enough fashion, 'Are you quite comfortable, sir?'

The Hawkinsite answered, 'Quite. Your wife has been most thoughtful in all her arrangements.'

'Would you care for a drink?'

The Hawkinsite did not answer but looked at Rose with a slight facial contortion that indicated some emotion which, unfortunately, Rose could not interpret. She said, nervously, 'On Earth there is the custom of drinking liquids which have been fortified with ethyl alcohol. We find it stimulating.'

'Oh, yes. I am afraid, then, that I must decline. Ethyl alcohol would interfere most unpleasantly with my metabolism.'

'Why, so it does to Earthmen, too, but I understand, Dr. Tholan,' Drake replied. 'Would you object to *my* drinking?'

'Of course not.'

Drake passed close to Rose on his way to the sideboard and she caught only one word. He said, 'God!' in a tightly controlled whisper, yet he managed to put seventeen exclamation points after it.

The Hawkinsite *stood* at the table. His fingers were models of dexterity as they wove their way around the cutlery. Rose tried not to look at him as he ate. His wide lipless mouth split his face alarmingly as he ingested food, and, in chewing, his large jaws moved disconcertingly from side to side. It was another evidence of his ungulate ancestry. Rose found herself wondering if, in the quiet of his own room, he would later chew his cud, and was then panic-stricken lest Drake get the same idea and leave the table in disgust. But Drake was taking everything quite calmly.

He said, 'I imagine, Dr. Tholan, that the cylinder at your side holds cyanide?'

Rose started. She had actually not noticed it. It was a curved metal object, something like a water canteen, that fitted flatly against the creature's skin, half-hidden behind its clothing. But, then, Drake had a policeman's eyes.

The Hawkinsite was not in the least disconcerted. 'Quite so,' he said, and his hoofed fingers held out a thin, flexible hose that ran up his body, its tint blending into that of his yellowish skin, and entered the corner of his wide mouth. Rose felt slightly embarrassed, as though at the display of intimate articles of clothing.

Drake said, 'And does it contain pure cyanide?'

The Hawkinsite humorously blinked his eyes. 'I hope you are not considering possible danger to Earthites. I know the gas is highly poisonous to you and I do not need a great deal. The gas contained in the cylinder is five per cent hydrogen cyanide, the remainder oxygen. None of it emerges except when I actually suck at the tube, and that need not be done frequently.'

'I see. And you really must have the gas to live?'

Rose was slightly appalled. One simply did not ask such questions without careful preparation. It was impossible to foresee where the sensitive points of an alien psychology might be. And Drake *must* be doing this deliberately, since he could not help realizing that he could get answers to such questions as easily from herself. Or was it that he preferred not to ask her?

The Hawkinsite remained apparently unperturbed. 'Are you not a biologist, Mr. Smollett?'

'No, Dr. Tholan.'

'But you are in close association with Mrs. *Dr.* Smollett.'

Drake smiled a bit. 'Yes, I am married to a Mrs. doctor, but just the same I am not a biologist; merely a minor government official. My wife's friends', added, 'call me a policeman.'

Rose bit the inside of her cheek. In this case it was the Hawkinsite who had impinged upon the sensitive point of an alien psychology. On Hawkin's Planet, there was a tight caste system and intercaste associations were limited. But Drake wouldn't realize that.

The Hawkinsite turned to her. 'May I have your permission, Mrs. Smollett, to explain a little of our biochemistry to your husband? It will be dull for you, since I am sure you must understand it quite well already.'

She said, 'By all means do, Dr. Tholan.'

He said, 'You see, Mr. Smollett, the respiratory system in your body and in the bodies of all air-breathing creatures on Earth is controlled by certain metal-containing enzymes, I am taught. The metal is usually iron, though sometimes it is copper. In either case, small traces of cyanide would combine with these metals and immobilize the respiratory system of the terrestrial living cell. They would be prevented from using oxygen and killed in a few minutes.

'The life on my own planet is not quite so constituted. The key respiratory compounds contain neither iron nor copper; no metal at all, in fact. It is for this reason that my blood is colorless. Our compounds contain certain organic groupings which are essential to life, and these groupings can only be maintained intact in the presence of a small concentration of cyanide. Undoubtedly, this type of protein has developed through millions of years of evolution on a world which has a few tenths of a per cent of hydrogen cyanide occurring naturally in the atmosphere. Its presence is maintained by a biological cycle. Various of our native micro-organisms liberate the free gas.'

'You make it extremely clear, Dr. Tholan, and very interesting,' Drake said. 'What happens if you don't breathe it? Do you just go, like that?' He snapped his fingers.

'Not quite. It isn't equivalent to the presence of cyanide for you. In my case, the absence of cyanide would be equivalent to slow strangulation. It happens sometimes, in ill-ventilated rooms on my world, that the cyanide is gradually consumed and falls below the minimum necessary concentration. The results are very painful and difficult to treat.'

Rose had to give Drake credit; he really sounded interested. And the alien, thank heaven, did not mind the catechism.

The rest of the dinner passed without incident. It was almost pleasant.

Throughout the evening, Drake remained that way; interested. Even more than that – absorbed. He drowned her out, and she was glad of it. *He* was the one who was really colorful and it was only her job, her specialized training, that stole the color from him. She looked at him gloomily and thought, *Why did he marry me?*

Drake sat, one leg crossed over the other, hands clasped and tapering his chin gently, watching the Hawkinsite intently. The Hawkinsite faced him, standing in his quadruped fashion.

Drake said, 'I find it difficult to keep thinking of you as a doctor.'

The Hawkinsite laughingly blinked his eyes. 'I understand what you mean,' he said. 'I find it difficult to think of you as a policeman. On my world, policemen are very specialized and distinctive people.'

'Are they?' said Drake, somewhat drily, and then changed the subject. 'I gather that you are not here on a pleasure trip.'

'No, I am here very much on business. I intend to study this queer planet you call Earth, as it has never been studied before by any of my people.'

'Queer?' asked Drake. 'In what way?'

The Hawkinsite looked at Rose. 'Does he know of the Inhibition Death?'

Rose felt embarrassed. 'His work is important,' she said. 'I am afraid that my husband has little time to listen to the details of my work.' She knew that this was not really adequate and she felt herself to be the recipient, yet again, of one of the Hawkinsite's unreadable emotions.

The extraterrestrial creature turned back to Drake. 'It is always amazing to me to find how little you Earthmen understand your own unusual characteristics. Look, there are five intelligent races in the Galaxy. These have all developed independently, yet have managed to converge in remarkable fashion. It is as though, in the long run, intelligence requires a certain physical makeup to flourish. I leave that question for philosophers. But I need not belabor the point, since it must be a familiar one to you.

'Now when the differences among the intelligences are closely investigated, it is found over and over again that it is you Earthmen, more than any of the others, who are unique. For instance, it is only on Earth that life depends upon metal enzymes for respirations. Your people are the only ones which find hydrogen cyanide poisonous. Yours is the only form of intelligent life which is carnivorous. Yours is the only form of life which has not developed from a grazing animal. And, most interesting of all, yours is the only form of intelligent life known which stops growing upon reaching maturity.'

Drake grinned at him. Rose felt her heart suddenly race. It was the nicest thing about him, that grin, and he was using it perfectly naturally. It wasn't forced or false. He was adjusting to the presence of this alien creature. He was being pleasant – and he must be doing it for her. She loved that thought and repeated it to herself. He was doing it for her; he was being nice to the Hawkinsite for her sake.

Drake was saying with his grin, 'You don't look very large, Dr. Tholan. I should say that you are an inch taller than I am, which would make you six feet two inches tall. Is it that you are young, or is it that the others on your world are generally small?'

'Neither,' said the Hawkinsite. 'We grow at a diminishing rate with the years, so that at my age it would take fifteen years to grow an additional inch, but – and this is the important point – we never *entirely* stop. And, of course, as a consequence, we never entirely die.'

Drake gasped and even Rose felt herself sitting stiffly upright. This was something new. This was something which, to her knowledge, the few expeditions to Hawkin's Planet had never brought back. She was torn with excitement but held an exclamation back and let Drake speak for her.

He said, 'They don't entirely die? You're not trying to say, sir, that the people on Hawkin's Planet are immortal?'

'No people are truly immortal. If there were no other way to die, there would always be accident, and if that fails, there is boredom. Few of us live more than several centuries of your time. Still, it is unpleasant to think that death may come involuntarily. It is something which, to us, is extremely horrible. It bothers me even as I think of it now, this thought that *against my will and despite all care,* death may come.'

'We,' said Drake, grimly, 'are quite used to it.'

'You Earthmen live with the thought; we do not. And this is

why we are disturbed to find that the incidence of Inhibition Death has been increasing in recent years.'

'You have not yet explained', said Drake, 'just what the Inhibition Death is, but let me guess. Is the Inhibition Death a pathological cessation of growth?'

'Exactly.'

'And how long after growth's cessation does death follow?'

'Within the year. It is a wasting disease, a tragic one, and absolutely incurable.'

'What causes it?'

The Hawkinsite paused a long time before answering, and even then there was something strained and uneasy about the way he spoke. 'Mr. Smollett, we know nothing about the cause of the disease.'

Drake nodded thoughtfully. Rose was following the conversation as though she were a spectator at a tennis match.

Drake said, 'And why do you come to Earth to study this disease?'

'Because again Earthmen are unique. They are the only intelligent beings who are immune. The Inhibition Death affects *all* the other races. Do your biologists know that, Mrs. Smollett?'

He had addressed her suddenly, so that she jumped slightly. She said, 'No, they don't.'

'I am not surprised. That piece of information is the result of very recent research. The Inhibition Death is easily diagnosed incorrectly and the incidence is much lower on the other planets. In fact, it is a strange thing, something to philosophize over, that the incidence of the Death is highest on my world, which is closest to Earth, and lower on each more distant planet – so that it is lowest on the world of the star Tempora, which is farthest from Earth, while Earth itself is immune. Somewhere in the biochemistry of the Earthite, there is the secret of that immunity. How interesting it would be to find it.'

Drake said, 'But look here, you can't say Earth is immune. From where I sit, it looks as if the incidence is a hundred per cent. All Earthmen stop growing and all Earthmen die. We've *all* got the Inhibition Death.'

'Not at all. Earthmen live up to seventy years after the cessation of growth. That is not the Death as *we* know it. *Your* equiva-

lent disease is rather one of unrestrained growth. Cancer, you call
it. – But come, I bore you.'

Rose protested instantly. Drake did likewise with even more
vehemence, but the Hawkinsite determinedly changed the subject. It was then that Rose had her first pang of suspicion, for
Drake circled Harg Tholan warily with his words, worrying him,
jabbing at him, attempting always to get the information back to
the point where the Hawkinsite had left off. Not baldly, not
unskilfully, but Rose knew him, and could tell what he was
after. And what could he be after but that which was demanded
by his profession? And, as though in response to her thoughts,
the Hawkinsite took up the phrase which had begun careening
in her mind like a broken record on a perpetual turntable.

He asked, 'Did you not say you were a policeman?'

Drake said, curtly, 'Yes.'

'Then there is something I would like to request you to do for
me. I have been wanting to all this evening, since I discovered
your profession, and yet I hesitate. I do not wish to be trouble-
some to my host and hostess.'

'We'll do what we can.'

'I have a profound curiousity as to how Earthmen live: a curiosity which is not perhaps shared by the generality of my coun-
trymen. So I wonder, could you show me through one of the
police departments on your planet?'

'I do not belong to a police department in exactly the way you
imagine,' said Drake, cautiously. 'However, I am known to the
New York police department. I can manage it without trouble.
Tomorrow?'

'That would be most convenient for me. Would I be able to
visit the Missing Persons Bureau?'

'The what?'

The Hawkinsite drew his four standing legs closer together,
as if he were becoming more intense. 'It is a hobby of mine, a little
queer corner of interest I have always had. I understand you
have a group of police officers whose sole duty it is to search for
men who are missing.'

'And women and children,' added Drake. 'But why should
that interest you so particularly?'

'Because there again you are unique. There is no such thing as
a missing person on our planet. I can't explain the mechanism

to you, of course, but among the people of other worlds, there is always an awareness of one another's presence, especially if there is a strong, affectionate tie. We are always aware of each other's exact location, no matter where on the planet we might be.'

Rose grew excited again. The scientific expeditions to Hawkin's Planet had always had the greatest difficulty in penetrating the internal emotional mechanisms of the natives, and here was one who talked freely, who would explain! She forgot to worry about Drake and intruded into the conversations. 'Can you feel such awareness even now? On Earth?'

The Hawkinsite said, 'You mean across space? No, I'm afraid not. But you see the importance of the matter. All the uniqueness of Earth should be linked. If the lack of this sense can be explained, perhaps the immunity to Inhibition Death can be, also. Besides, it strikes me as very curious that any form of intelligent community life can be built among people who lack this community awareness. How can an Earthman tell, for instance, when he has formed a congenial sub-group, a family? How can you two, for instance, know that there is a true tie between you?'

Rose found herself nodding. How strongly she missed such a sense!

But Drake only smiled. 'We have our ways. It is as difficult to explain what we call "love" to you as it is for you to explain your sense to us.'

'I suppose so. Yet tell me truthfully, Mr. Smollett – if Mrs. Smollett were to leave this room and enter another without your having seen her do so, would you really not be aware of her location?'

'I really would not.'

The Hawkinsite said, 'Amazing.' He hesitated, then added, 'Please do not be offended at the fact that I find it revolting as well.'

After the light in the bedroom had been put out, Rose went to the door three times, opening it a crack and peering out. She could feel Drake watching her. There was a hard kind of amusement in his voice as he asked, finally, 'What's the matter?'

She said, 'I want to talk to you.'

'Are you afraid our friend can hear?'

Rose was whispering. She got into bed and put her head on his pillow so that she could whisper better. She said, 'Why were you talking about the Inhibition Death to Dr. Tholan?'

'I am taking an interest in your work, Rose. You've always wanted me to take an interest.'

'I'd rather you weren't sarcastic.' She was almost violent, as nearly violent as she could be in a whisper. 'I know that there's something of your own interest in this – of *police* interest, probably. What is it?'

He said, 'I'll talk to you tomorrow.'

'No, right now.'

He put his hand under her head, lifting it. For a wild moment she thought he was going to kiss her – just kiss her on impulse the way husbands sometimes did, or as she imagined they sometime did. Drake never did, and he didn't now.

He merely held her close and whispered, 'Why are you so interested?'

His hand was almost brutally hard upon the nape of her neck, so that she stiffened and tried to draw back. Her voice was more than a whisper now. 'Stop it, Drake.'

He said, 'I want no questions from you and no interference. You do your job, and I'll do mine.'

'The nature of my job is open and known.'

'The nature of my job', he retorted. 'isn't, by definition. But I'll tell you this. Our six-legged friend is here in this house for some definite reason. You weren't picked as biologist in charge for any random reason. Do you know that two days ago, he'd been inquiring about me at the Commission?'

'You're joking.'

'Don't believe that for a minute. There are depths to this that you know nothing about. But that's my job and I won't discuss it with you any further. Do you understand?'

'No, but I won't question you if you don't want me to.'

'Then go to sleep.'

She lay stiffly on her back and the minutes passed, and then the quarter-hours. She was trying to fit the pieces together. Even with what Drake had told her, the curves and colors refused to blend. She wondered what Drake would say if he knew she had a recording of that night's conversation!

One picture remained clear in her mind at that moment. It hovered over her mockingly. The Hawkinsite, at the end of the long evening, had turned to her and said gravely, 'Good night, Mrs. Smollet. You are a most charming hostess.'

She had desperately wanted to giggle at the time. How could he call her a charming hostess? To him, she could only be a horror, a monstrosity with too few limbs and a too-narrow face.

And then, as the Hawkinsite delivered himself of this completely meaningless piece of politeness, Drake had turned white! For one instant, his eyes had burned with something that looked like terror.

She had never before known Drake to show fear of anything, and the picture of that instant of pure panic remained with her until all her thoughts finally sagged into the oblivion of sleep.

It was noon before Rose was at her desk the next day. She had deliberately waited until Drake and the Hawkinsite had left, since only then was she able to remove the small recorder that had been behind Drake's armchair the previous evening. She had had no original intention of keeping its presence secret from him. It was just that he had come home so late, and she couldn't say anything about it with the Hawkinsite present. Later on, of course, things had changed –

The placing of the recorder had been only a routine maneuver. The Hawkinsite's statements and intonations needed to be preserved for future intensive studies by various specialists at the Institute. It had been hidden in order to avoid the distortions of self-consciousness that the visibility of such a device would bring, and now it couldn't be shown to the members of the Institute at all. It would have to serve a different function altogether. A rather nasty function.

She was going to spy on Drake.

She touched the little box with her fingers and wondered, irrelevantly, how Drake was going to manage, that day. Social intercourse between inhabited worlds was, even now, not so commonplace that the sight of a Hawkinsite on the city streets would not succeed in drawing crowds. But Drake would manage, she knew. Drake always managed.

She listened once again to the sounds of last evening, repeating the interesting moments. She was dissatisfied with what Drake had told her. Why should the Hawkinsite have been interested in the two of them particularly? Yet Drake wouldn't lie. She would have liked to check at the Security Commission,

but she knew she could not do that. Besides, the thought made
her feel disloyal; Drake would definitely not lie.

But, then again, why should Harg Tholan not have investigated them? He might have inquired similarly about the families
of all the biologists at the Institute. It would be no more than
natural to attempt to choose the home he would find most
pleasant by his own standards, whatever they were.

And if he had — even if he had investigated only the Smoll-
etts — why should that create the great change in Drake from
intense hostility to intense interest? Drake undoubtedly had
knowledge he was keeping to himself. Only heaven knew how
much.

Her thoughts churned slowly through the possibilities of interstellar intrigue. So far, to be sure, there were no signs of hostility or ill-feeling among any of the five intelligent races known
to inhabit the Galaxy. As yet they were spaced at intervals too
wide for enmity. Even the barest contact among them was all
but impossible. Economic and political interests just had no
point at which to conflict.

But that was only her idea and she was not a member of the
Security Commission. If there *were* conflict, if there *were* dan-
ger, if there *were* any reason to suspect that the mission of a
Hawkinsite might be other than peaceful — Drake would know.

Yet was Drake sufficiently high in the councils of the Security
Commission to know, off-hand, the dangers involved in the visit
of a Hawkinsite physician? She had never thought of his position as more than that of a very minor functionary in the Commission; he had never presented himself as more. And yet —

Might he be more?

She shrugged at the thought. It was reminiscent of twentieth-
century spy novels and of costume dramas of the days when
there existed such things as atom bomb secrets.

The thought of costume dramas decided her. Unlike Drake,
she wasn't a real policeman, and she didn't know how a real
policeman would go about it. But she knew how such things
were done in the old dramas.

She drew a piece of paper toward her and, with a quick motion, slashed a vertical pencil mark down its center. She headed
one column 'Harg Tholan', the other 'Drake'. Under 'Harg Tholan' she wrote 'bona fide' and thoughtfully put three question
marks after it. After all, was he a doctor at all, or was he what

could only be described as an interstellar agent? What proof had even the Institute of his profession except his own statements? Was that why Drake had quizzed him so relentlessly concerning the Inhibition Death? Had he boned up in advance and tried to catch the Hawkinsite in an error?

For a moment, she was irresolute; then, springing to her feet, she folded the paper, put it in the pocket of her short jacket, and swept out of her office. She said nothing to any of those she passed as she left the Institute. She left no word at the reception desk as to where she was going, or when she would be back.

Once outside, she hurried into the third-level tube and waited for an empty compartment to pass. The two minutes that elapsed seemed unbearably long. It was all she could do to say, 'New York Academy of Medicine,' into the mouthpiece just above the seat.

The door of the little cubicle closed, and the sound of the air flowing past the compartment hissed upward in pitch.

The New York Academy of Medicine had been enlarged both vertically and horizontally in the past two decades. The library alone occupied one entire wing of the third floor. Undoubtedly, if all the books, pamphlets and periodicals it contained were in their original printed form, rather than in microfilm, the entire building, huge though it was, would not have been sufficiently vast to hold them. As it was, Rose knew there was already talk of limiting printed works to the last five years, rather than to the last ten, as was now the case.

Rose, as a member of the Academy, had free entry to the library. She hurried toward the alcoves devoted to extraterrestrial medicine and was relieved to find them unoccupied.

It might have been wiser to have enlisted the aid of a librarian, but she chose not to. The thinner and smaller the trail she left, the less likely it was that Drake might pick it up.

And so, without guidance, she was satisfied to travel along the shelves, following the titles anxiously with her fingers. The books were almost all in English, though some were in German or Russian. None, ironically enough, were in extraterrestrial symbolisms. There was a room somewhere for such originals, but they were available only to official translators.

Her traveling eye and finger stopped. She had found what she was looking for.

She dragged half a dozen volumes from the shelf and spread

them out upon the small dark table. She fumbled for the light
switch and opened the first of the volumes. It was entitled *Studies on Inhibition*. She leafed through it and then turned to the
author index. The name of Harg Tholan was there.

One by one, she looked up the references indicated, then returned to the shelves for translations of such original papers as
she could find.

She spent more than two hours in the Academy. When she
was finished, she knew this much — there was a Hawkinsite doctor named Harg Tholan, who was an expert on the Inhibition
Death. He was connected with the Hawkinsite research organization with which the Institute had been in correspondence. Of
course, the Harg Tholan she knew might simply be impersonat-
ing an actual doctor to make the role more realistic, but why
should that be necessary?

She took the paper out of her pocket and, where she had written 'bona fide' with three question marks, she now wrote a YES
in capitals. She went back to the Institute and at 4 p.m. was once
again at her desk. She called the switchboard to say that she
would not answer any phone calls and then she locked her door.

Underneath the column headed 'Harg Tholan' she now wrote
two questions: 'Why did Harg Tholan come to Earth alone?'
She left considerable space. Then, 'What is his interest in the
Missing Persons Bureau?'

Certainly, the Inhibition Death was all the Hawkinsite said it
was. From her reading at the Academy, it was obvious that it
occupied the major share of medical effort on Hawkin's Planet.
It was more feared there than cancer was on Earth. If they had
thought the answer to it lay on Earth, the Hawkinsites would
have sent a full-scale expedition. Was it distrust and suspicion
on their part that made them send only one investigator?

What was it Harg Tholan had said the night before? The incidence of the Death was highest upon his own world, which was
closest to Earth, lowest upon the world farthest from Earth. Add
to that the fact implied by the Hawkinsite, and verified by her
own readings at the Academy, that the incidence had expanded
enormously since interstellar contact had been made with
Earth. . . .

Slowly and reluctantly she came to one conclusion. The in-
habitants of Hawkin's Planet might have decided that somehow

Earth had discovered the cause of the Inhibition Death, and was deliberately fostering it among the alien peoples of the Galaxy, with the intention, perhaps, of becoming supreme among the stars.

She rejected this conclusion with what was almost panic. It could not be; it was impossible. In the first place, Earth *wouldn't* do such a horrible thing. Secondly, it *couldn't*.

As far as scientific advance was concerned, the beings of Hawkin's Planet were certainly the equals of Earthmen. The Death had occurred there for thousands of years and their medical record was one of total failure. Surely, Earth, in its long-distance investigations into alien biochemistry, could not have succeeded so quickly. In fact, as far as she knew, there were no investigations to speak of into Hawkinsite pathology on the part of Earth biologists and physicians.

Yet all the evidence indicated that Harg Tholan had come in suspicion and had been received in suspicion. Carefully, she wrote down under the question, 'Why did Harg Tholan come to Earth alone?' the answer, 'Hawkin's Planet *believes* Earth is causing the Inhibition Death.'

But, then, what was this business about the Bureau of Missing Persons? As a scientist, she was rigorous about the theories she developed. *All* the facts had to fit in, not merely some of them.

Missing Persons Bureau! If it was a false trail, deliberately intended to deceive Drake, it had been done clumsily, since it came only after an hour of discussion of the Inhibition Death.

Was it intended as an opportunity to study Drake? If so, why? Was this perhaps the *major* point? The Hawkinsite had investigated Drake before coming to them. Had he come because Drake was a policeman with entry to Bureaux of Missing Persons?

But why? Why?

She gave it up and turned to the column headed 'Drake'.

And there a question wrote itself, not in pen and ink upon the paper, but in the much more visible letters of thought on mind. *Why did he marry me?* thought Rose, and she covered her eyes with her hands so that the unfriendly light was excluded.

They had met quite by accident somewhat more than a year before, when he had moved into the apartment house in which she then lived. Polite greetings had somehow become friendly conversation and this, in turn, had led to occasional dinners in a neighborhood restaurant. It had been very friendly and normal and an exciting new experience, and she had fallen in love.

When he asked her to marry him, she was pleased – and over-whelmed. At the time, she had many explanations for it. He appreciated her intelligence and friendliness. She was a nice girl. She would make a good wife, a splendid companion.

She had tried all those explanations and had half-believed every one of them. But half-belief was not enough.

It was not that she had any definite fault to find in Drake as a husband He was always thoughtful, kind and a gentleman. Their married life was not one of passion, and yet it suited the paler emotional surges of the late thirties. She wasn't nineteen. What did she expect?

That was it; she wasn't nineteen. She wasn't beautiful, or charming, or glamorous. What did she expect? Could she have expected Drake – handsome and rugged, whose interest in intel-lectual pursuits was quite minor, who neither asked about her work in all the months of their marriage, nor offered to discuss his own with her? Why, then, did he marry her?

But there was no answer to that question, and it had nothing to do with what Rose was trying to do now. It was extraneous, she told herself fiercely; it was a childish distraction from the task she had set herself. She was acting like a girl of nineteen, after all, with no chronological excuse for it.

She found that the point of her pencil had somehow broken, and took a new one. In the column headed 'Drake' she wrote, 'Why is he suspicious of Harg Tholan?' and under it she put an arrow pointing to the other column.

What she had already written there was sufficient explanation. If Earth was spreading the Inhibition Death, or if Earth knew it was suspected of such a deed, then, obviously, it would be preparing for eventual retaliation on the part of the aliens. In fact, the setting would actually be one of preliminary maneuver-ing for the first interstellar war of history. It was an adequate but horrible explanation.

Now there was left the second question, the one she could not answer. She wrote it slowly, 'Why Drake's reaction to Tholan's words, "You are a most charming hostess"?'

She tried to bring back the exact setting. The Hawkinsite had said it innocuously, matter-of-factly, politely, and Drake had frozen at the sound of it. Over and over, she had listened to that particular passage in the recording. An Earthman might have said it in just such an inconsequential tone on leaving a routine cocktail party. The recording did not carry the sight of Drake's face; she had only her memory for that. Drake's eyes had become alive with fear and hate, and Drake was one who feared practically nothing. What was there to fear in the phrase, 'You are a most charming hostess', that could upset him so? Jealousy? Absurd. The feeling that Tholan had been sarcastic? Maybe, though unlikely. She was sure Tholan was sincere.

She gave it up and put a large question mark under that second question. There were two of them now, one under 'Harg Tholan' and one under 'Drake'. Could there be a connection between Tholan's interest in missing persons and Drake's reaction to a polite party phrase? She could think of none.

She put her head down upon her arms. It was getting dark in the office and she was very tired. For a while, she must have hovered in that queer land between waking and sleeping, when thoughts and phrases lose the control of the conscious and disport themselves erratically and surrealistically through one's head. But, no matter where they danced and leaped, they always returned to that one phrase, 'You are a most charming hostess.' Sometimes she heard it in Harg Tholan's cultured, lifeless voice, and sometimes in Drake's vibrant one. When Drake said it, it was full of love, full of a love she never heard from him. She liked to hear him say it.

She startled herself to wakefulness. It was quite dark in the office now, and she put on the desk light. She blinked, then frowned a little. Another thought must have come to her in that fitful half-sleep. There had been another phrase which had upset Drake. What was it? Her forehead furrowed with mental effort. It had not been last evening. It was not anything in the recorded conversation, so it must have been before that. Nothing came and she grew restless.

Looking at her watch, she gasped. It was almost eight. They would be at home waiting for her.

But she did not want to go home. She did not want to face them. Slowly, she took up the paper upon which she had scrawled her thoughts of the afternoon, tore it into little pieces and let them flutter into the little atomic-flash ashtray upon her desk. They were gone in a little flare and nothing was left of them.

If only nothing were left of the thoughts they represented as well.

It was no use. She would have to go home.

They were not there waiting for her, after all. She came upon them getting out of a gyrocab just as she emerged from the tubes on to street level. The gyrocabbie, wide-eyed, gazed after his fares for a moment, then hovered upward and away. By unspoken mutual consent, the three waited until they had entered the apartment before speaking.

Rose said disinterestedly, 'I hope you have had a pleasant day, Dr. Tholan.'

'Quite. And a fascinating and profitable one as well, I think.'

'Have you had a chance to eat?' Though Rose had not herself eaten, she was anything but hungry.

'Yes, indeed.'

Drake interrupted, 'We had lunch and supper sent up to us. Sandwiches.' He sounded tired.

Rose said, 'Hello, Drake.' It was the first time she had addressed him.

Drake scarcely looked at her. 'Hello.'

The Hawkinsite said, 'Your tomatoes are remarkable vegetables. We have nothing to compare with them in taste on our own planet. I believe I ate two dozen, as well as an entire bottle of tomato derivative.'

'Ketchup,' explained Drake, briefly.

Rose said, 'And your visit at the Missing Persons Bureau, Dr. Tholan? You say you found it profitable?'

'I should say so. Yes.'

Rose kept her back to him. She plumped up sofa cushions as she said, 'In what way?'

'I find it most interesting that the large majority of missing persons are males. Wives frequently report missing husbands, while the reverse is practically never the case.'

Rose said, 'Oh, that's not mysterious, Dr. Tholan. You simply don't realize the economic setup we have on Earth. On this planet, you see, it is the male who is usually the member of the family that maintains it as an economic unit. He is the one whose labor is repaid in units of currency. The wife's function is generally that of taking care of home and children.'

'Surely this is not universal!'

Drake put in, 'More or less. If you are thinking of my wife, she is an example of the minority of women who are capable of making their own way in the world.'

Rose looked at him swiftly. Was he being sarcastic?

The Hawkinsite said, 'Your implication, Mrs. Smollett, is that women, being economically dependent upon their male companions, find it less feasible to disappear?'

'That's a gentle way of putting it,' said Rose, 'but that's about it.'

'And would you call the Missing Persons Bureau of New York a fair sampling of such cases in the planet at large?'

'Why, I should think so.'

The Hawkinsite said, abruptly, 'And is there, then, an economic explanation for the fact that since interstellar travel has been developed, the percentage of young males among the missing is more pronounced than ever?'

It was Drake who answered, with a verbal snap. 'Good lord, that's even less of a mystery than the other. Nowadays, the runaway has all space to disappear into. Anyone who wants to get away from trouble need only hop the nearest space freighter. They're always looking for crewmen, no questions asked, and it would be almost impossible to locate the runaway after that, if he really wanted to stay out of circulation.'

'And almost always young men in their first year of marriage.'

Rose laughed suddenly. She said, 'Why, that's just the time a man's troubles seem the greatest. If he survives the first year, there is usually no need to disappear at all.'

Drake was obviously not amused. Rose thought again that he looked tired and unhappy. *Why* did he insist on bearing the load alone? And then she thought that perhaps he had to.

The Hawkinsite said, suddenly, "Would it offend you if I disconnected for a period of time?'

Rose said, 'Not at all. I hope you haven't had too exhausting a day. Since you come from a planet whose gravity is greater than that of Earth's, I'm afraid we too easily presume that you would show greater endurance than we do.'

'Oh, I am not tired in a physical sense.' He looked for a moment at her legs and blinked very rapidly, indicating amusement. 'You know, I keep expecting Earthmen to fall either forward or backward in view of their meager equipment of standing limbs.

You must pardon me if my comment is overfamiliar, but your mention of the lesser gravity of Earth brought it to my mind. On my planet, two legs would simply not be enough. But this is all beside the point at the moment. It is just that I have been absorbing so many new and unusual concepts that I feel the desire for a little disconnection.'

Rose shrugged inwardly. Well, that was as close as one race could get to another, anyway. As nearly as the expeditions to Hawkin's Planet could make out, Hawkinsites had the faculty for disconnecting their conscious mind from all its bodily functions and allowing it to sink into an undisturbed meditative process for periods of time lasting up to terrestrial days. Hawkinsites found the process pleasant, even necessary sometimes, though no Earthman could truly say what function it served.

Conversely, it had never been entirely possible for Earthmen to explain the concept of 'sleep' to a Hawkinsite, or to any extra-terrestrial. What an Earthman would call sleep or a dream, a Hawkinsite would view as an alarming sign of mental disintegration.

Rose thought uneasily, *Here is another way Earthmen are unique.*

The Hawkinsite was backing away, drooping so that his fore-limbs swept the floor in polite farewell. Drake nodded curtly at him as he disappeared behind the bend in the corridor. They heard his door open, close, then silence.

After minutes in which the silence was thick between them, Drake's chair creaked as he shifted restlessly. With a mild horror, Rose noticed blood upon his lips. She thought to herself, *He's in some kind of trouble. I've got to talk to him. I can't let it go on like this.*

She said, 'Drake!'

Drake seemed to look at her from a far, far distance. Slowly, his eyes focused closer at hand and he said, 'What is it? Are you through for the day, too?'

'No, I'm ready to begin. It's the tomorrow you spoke of. Aren't you going to speak to me?'

'Pardon me?'

'Last night, you said you would speak to me tomorrow. I am ready now.'

Drake frowned. His eyes withdrew beneath a lowered brow and Rose felt some of her resolution begin to leave her. He said, 'I thought it was agreed that you would not question me about my business in this matter.'

'I think it's too late for that. I know too much about your business by now.'

'What do you mean?' he shouted, jumping to his feet. Recollecting himself, he approached, laid his hands upon her shoulders and repeated in a lower voice, 'What do you mean?'

Rose kept her eyes upon her hands, which rested limply in her lap. She bore the painfully gripping fingers patiently, and said slowly, 'Dr. Tholan thinks that Earth is spreading the Inhibition Death purposely. That's it, isn't it?'

She waited. Slowly, the grip relaxed and he was standing there, hands at his sides, face baffled and unhappy. He said, 'Where did you get that notion?'

'It's true, isn't it?'

He said breathlessly, unnaturally, 'I want to know exactly why you say that. Don't play foolish games with me, Rose. This is for keeps.'

'If I tell you, will you answer one question?'

'What question?'

'Is Earth spreading the disease deliberately, Drake?'

Drake flung his hands upward. 'Oh, for Heaven's sake!'

He knelt before her. He took both her hands in his and she could feel their trembling. He was forcing his voice into soothing, loving syllables.

He was saying, 'Rose dear, look, you've got something red-hot by the tail and you think you can use it to tease me in a little husband-wife repartee. No, I'm not asking much. Just tell me exactly what causes you to say what – what you have just said.' He was terrible earnest about it.

'I was at the New York Academy of Medicine this afternoon. I did some reading there.'

'But why? What made you do it?'

'You seemed so interested in the Inhibition Death, for one thing. And Dr. Tholan made those statements about the incidence increasing since interstellar travel, and being the highest on the planet nearest Earth.' She paused.

'And your reading?' he prompted. 'What about your reading, Rose?'

She said, 'It backs him up. All I could do was to skim hastily into the direction of their research in recent decades. It seems obvious to me, though, that at least some of the Hawkinsites are considering the possibility the Inhibition Death originates on Earth.'

'Do they say so outright?'

'No. Or, if they have, I haven't seen it.' She gazed at him in surprise. In a matter like this, certainly the government would have investigated Hawkinsite research on the matter. She said, gently, 'Don't you know about Hawkinsite research in the matter, Drake? The government –'

'Never mind about that.' Drake had moved away from her and now he turned again. His eyes were bright. He said, as though making a wonderful discovery, 'Why, you're an expert in this!'

Was she? Did he find that out only now that he needed her? Her nostrils flared and she said flatly, 'I am a biologist.'

He said, 'Yes, I know that, but I mean your particular speciality is growth. Didn't you once tell me you had done work on growth?'

'You might call it that. I've had twenty papers published on the relationship of nucleic acid fine structure and embryonic development on my Cancer Society grant.'

'Good. I should have thought of that.' He was choked with a new excitement. 'Tell me, Rose – Look, I'm sorry if I lost my temper with you a moment ago. You'd be as competent as anyone to understand the direction of their researches if you read about it, wouldn't you?'

'Fairly competent, yes.'

'Then tell me how they think the disease is spread. The details, I mean.'

'Oh, now look, that's asking a little too much. I spent a few hours in the Academy, that's all. I'd need much more time than that to be able to answer your question.'

'An intelligent guess, at least. You can't imagine how important it is.'

She said, doubtfully, 'Of course, "Studies on Inhibition" is a major treatise in the field. It would summarize all of the available research data.'

'Yes? And how recent is it?'

'It's one of those periodic things. The last volume is about a year old.'

'Does it have any account of *his* work in it?' His finger jabbed in the direction of Harg Tholan's bedroom.

'More than anyone else's. He's an outstanding worker in the field. I looked over his papers especially.'

'And what are his theories about the origin of the disease? Try to remember, Rose.'

She shook her head at him. 'I could swear he blames Earth, but he admits they know nothing about how the disease is spread. I could swear to that, too.'

He stood stiffly before her. His strong hands were clenched into fists at his sides and his words were scarcely more than a mutter. 'It could be a matter of complete overestimation. Who knows —'

He whirled away. 'I'll find out about this right now, Rose. Thank you for your help.'

She ran after him. 'What are you going to do?'

'Ask him a few questions.' He was rummaging through the drawers of his desk and now his right hand withdrew. It held a needle-gun.

She cried, 'No, Drake!'

He shook her off roughly, and turned down the corridor toward the Hawkinsite's bedroom.

Drake threw the door open and entered. Rose was at his heels, still trying to grasp his arm, but now he stopped and looked at Harg Tholan.

The Hawkinsite was standing there motionless, eyes unfocused, his four standing limps sprawled out in four directions as far as they would go. Rose felt ashamed of intruding, as though she were violating an intimate rite. But Drake, apparently unconcerned, walked to within four feet of the creature and stood there. They were face to face, Drake holding the needle-gun easily at a level of about the center of the Hawkinsite's torso.

Drake said, 'Now keep quiet. He'll gradually become aware of me.'

'How do you know?'

The answer was flat. 'I *know*. Now get out of here.'

But she did not move and Drake was too absorbed to pay her further attention.

Portions of the skin on the Hawkinsite's face were beginning to quiver slightly. It was rather repulsive and Rose found herself preferring not to watch.

Drake said suddenly, 'That's about all, Dr. Tholan. Don't throw in connection with any of the limbs. Your sense organs and voice box will be quite enough.'

The Hawkinsite's voice was dim. 'Why do you invade my disconnection chamber?' Then, more strongly, 'And why are you armed?'

His head wobbled slightly atop a still frozen torso. He had, apparently, followed Drake's suggestion against limb connection. Rose wondered how Drake knew such partial reconnection to be possible. She herself had not known of it.

The Hawkinsite spoke again. 'What do you want?'

And this time Drake answered. He said, 'The answer to certain questions.'

'With a gun in your hand? I would not humor your discourtesy so far.'

'You would not merely be humoring me. You might be saving your own life.'

'That would be a matter of considerable indifference to me, under the circumstances. I am sorry, Mr. Smollett, that the duties toward a guest are so badly understood on Earth.'

'You are no guest of mine, Dr. Tholan,' said Drake. 'You entered my house on false pretenses. You had some reason for it, some way you had planned of using me to further your own purposes. I have no compunction in reversing the process.'

'You had better shoot. It will save time.'

'You are convinced that you will answer no questions? That, in itself, is suspicious. It seems that you consider certain answers to be more important than your life.'

'I consider the principles of courtesy to be very important. You, as an Earthman, may not understand.'

'Perhaps not. But I, as an Earthman, understand one thing.' Drake had jumped forward, faster than Rose could cry out, faster than the Hawkinsite could connect his limbs. When he sprang backward, the flexible hose of Harg Tholan's cyanide cylinder was in his hand. At the corner of the Hawkinsite's wide mouth, where the hose had once been affixed, a droplet of colorless liquid oozed sluggishly from a break in the rough skin, and slowly solidified into a brown jellylike globule, as it oxidized.

Drake yanked at the hose and the cylinder jerked free. He plunged home the knob that controlled the needle valve at the head of the cylinder and the small hissing ceased.

'I doubt', said Drake, 'that enough will have escaped to endanger us. I hope, however, that you realize what will happen to you *now,* if you do not answer the questions I am going to ask you – and answer them in such a way that I am convinced you are being truthful.'

'Give me back my cylinder,' said the Hawkinsite, slowly. 'If not, it will be necessary for me to attack you and then it will be necessary for you to kill me.'

Drake stepped back. 'Not at all. Attack me and I shoot your legs from under you. You will lose them; all four, if necessary, but you will still live, in a horrible way. You will live to die of cyanide lack. It would be a most uncomfortable death. I am only an Earthman and I can't appreciate its true horrors, but you can, can't you?'

The Hawkinsite's mouth was open and something within quivered yellow-green. Rose wanted to throw up. She wanted to scream, *Give him back the cylinder, Drake*! But nothing would come. She couldn't even turn her head.

Drake said, 'You have about an hour, I think, before the effects are irreversible. Talk quickly, Dr. Tholan, and you will have your cylinder back.'

'And after that –' said the Hawkinsite.

'After that, what does it matter to you? Even if I kill you then, it will be a clean death; not cyanide lack.'

Something seemed to pass out of the Hawkinsite. His voice grew guttural and his words blurred as though he no longer had the energy to keep his English perfect. He said, 'What are your questions?' and as he spoke, his eyes followed the cylinder in Drake's hand.

Drake swung it deliberately, tantalizingly, and the creature's eyes followed – followed –

Drake said, 'What are your theories concerning the Inhibition Death? Why did you really come to Earth? What is your interest in the Missing Persons Bureau?'

Rose found herself waiting in breathless anxiety. These were the questions she would like to have asked, too. Not in this manner, perhaps, but in Drake's job, kindness and humanity had to take second place to necessity.

She repeated that to herself several times in an effort to counteract the fact that she found herself loathing Drake for what he was doing to Dr. Tholan.

The Hawkinsite said, 'The proper answer would take more than the hour I have left me. You have bitterly shamed me by forcing me to talk under duress. On my own planet, you could not have done so under any circumstances. It is only here, on this revolting planet, that I can be deprived of cyanide.'

'You are wasting your hour, Dr. Tholan.'

'I would have told you this eventually, Mr. Smollett. I needed your help. It is why I came here.'

'You are still not answering my questions.'

'I will answer them now. For years, in addition to my regular scientific work, I have been privately investigating the cells of my patients suffering from Inhibition Death. I have been forced to use the utmost secrecy and to work without assistance, since the methods I used to investigate the bodies of my patients were frowned upon by my people. Your society would have similar feelings against human vivisection, for instance. For this reason, I could not present the results I obtained to my fellow physicians until I had verified my theories here on Earth.'

'What were your theories?' demanded Drake. The feverishness had returned to his eyes.

'It became more and more obvious to me as I proceeded with my studies that the entire direction of research into the Inhibition Death was wrong. Physically, there was no solution to its mystery. The Inhibition Death is entirely a disease of the mind.'

Rose interrupted, 'Surely, Dr. Tholan, it isn't psychosomatic.'

A thin, gray translucent film had passed over the Hawkinsite's eyes. He no longer looked at them. He said, 'No, Mrs. Smollett, it is not psychosomatic. It is a true disease of the mind; a mental infection. My patients had double minds. Beyond and beneath the one that obviously belonged to them, there was evidence of *another* one – an *alien* mind. I worked with Inhibition Death patients of other races than my own, and the same could be found. In short, there are not five intelligences in the Galaxy, but six. And the sixth is parasitic.'

Rose said, 'This is wild – impossible! You must be mistaken, Dr. Tholan.'

'I am not mistaken. Until I came to Earth, I thought I might be. But my stay at the Institute and my researches at the Missing

Persons Bureau convinced me that is not so. What is so impossible about the concept of a parasitic intelligence? Intelligences like these would not leave fossil remains, nor even leave artifacts – if their only function is to derive nourishment somehow from the mental activities of other creatures. One can imagine such a parasite, through the course of millions of years, perhaps, losing all portions of its physical being but that which remains necessary, just as a tapeworm, among your Earthly physical parasites, eventually lost all its functions but the single one of reproduction. In the case of the parasitic intelligence, all physical attributes would eventually be lost. It would become nothing but pure mind, living in some mental fashion we cannot conceive of on the minds of others. Particularly on the minds of Earthmen.'

Rose said, 'Why particularly Earthmen?'

Drake simply stood apart, intent, asking no further questions. He was content, apparently, to let the Hawkinsite speak.

'Have you not surmised that the sixth intelligence is a native of Earth? Mankind from the beginning has lived with it, has adapted to it, is unconscious of it. It is why the higher species of terrestrial animals, including man, do not grow after maturity and, eventually, die what is called natural death. It is the result of this universal parasitic infestation. It is why you sleep and dream, since it is then that the parasitic mind must feed and then that you are a little more conscious of it, perhaps. It is why the terrestrial mind alone of the intelligences is so subject to instability. Where else in the Galaxy are found split personalities and other such manifestations? After all, even now there must be occasional human minds which are visibly harmed by the presence of the parasite.

'Somehow, these parasitic minds could traverse space. They had no physical limitations. They could drift between the stars in what would correspond to a state of hibernation. Why the first ones did it, I don't know; probably no one will ever know. But once those first discovered the presence of intelligence on other planets in the Galaxy, there was a small, steady stream of parasitic intelligences making their way through space. We of the outer worlds must have been a gourmet's dish for them or they would have never struggled so hard to get to us. I imagine many must have failed to make the trip, but it must have been worth the effort to those who succeeded.

'But you see, we of the other worlds had not lived with these parasites for millions of years, as man and his ancestors had. We had not adapted ourselves to it. Our weak strains had not been killed off gradually through hundreds of generations until only the resistants were left. So, where Earthmen could survive the infection for decades with little harm, we others die a quick death within a year.'

'And is that why the incidence has increased since interstellar travel between Earth and the other planets has begun?'

'Yes.' For a moment there was silence, and then the Hawkinsite said with a sudden access of energy, 'Give me back my cylinder. You have your answer.'

Drake said coolly, 'What about the Missing Persons Bureau?' He was swinging the cylinder again; but now the Hawkinsite did not follow its movements. The gray translucent film on his eyes had deepened and Rose wondered whether that was simply an expression of weariness or an example of the changes induced by cyanide lack.

The Hawkinsite said, 'As we are not well adapted to the intelligence that infests man, neither is it well adapted to us. It can live on us – it even prefers to, apparently – but it cannot reproduce with ourselves alone as the source of its life. The Inhibition Death is therefore not directly contagious among our people.'

Rose looked at him with growing horror. 'What are you implying, Dr. Tholan?'

'The Earthman remains the prime host for the parasite. An Earthman may infect one of us if he remains among us. But the parasite, once it is located in an intelligence of the outer worlds, must somehow return to an Earthman, if it expects to reproduce. Before interstellar travel, this was possible only by a re-passage of space and therefore the incidence of infection remained infinitesimal. Now we are infected and reinfected as the parasites return to Earth and come back to us via the mind of Earthmen who travel through space.'

Rose said faintly, 'And the missing persons –'

'Are the intermediate hosts. The exact process by which it is done, I, of course, do not know. The masculine terrestrial mind seems better suited for their purposes. You'll remember that at the Institute I was told that the life expectancy of the average human male is three years less than that of the average female. Once reproduction has been taken care of, the infected male leaves, by spaceship, for the outer worlds. He disappears.'

'But this is impossible,' insisted Rose. 'What you say implies that the parasite mind can control the actions of its host! This cannot be, or we of Earth would have noticed their presence.'

'The control, Mrs. Smollett, may be very subtle, and may, moreover, be exerted only during the period of active reproduction. I simply point to your Missing Persons Bureau. Why do the young men disappear? You have economic and psychological explanations, but they are not sufficient. – But I am quite ill now and cannot speak much longer. I have only this to say. In the mental parasite, your people and mine have a common enemy. Earthmen, too, need not die involuntarily, except for its presence. I thought that if I found myself unable to return to my own world with my information because of the unorthodox methods I used to obtain it, I might bring it to the authorities on Earth, and ask their help in stamping out this menace. Imagine my pleasure when I found that the husband of one of the biologists at the Institute was a member of one of Earth's most important investigating bodies. Naturally, I did what I could to be made a guest at his home in order that I might deal with him privately; convince him of the terrible truth; utilize his position to help in the attack on the parasites.

'This is, of course, now impossible. I cannot blame you too far. As Earthmen, you cannot be expected to understand the psychology of my people. Nevertheless, you must understand this. I can have no further dealings with either of you. I could not even bear to remain any longer on Earth.'

Drake said, 'Then you alone, of all your people, have any knowledge of this theory of yours.'

'I alone.'

Drake held out the cylinder. 'Your cyanide, Dr. Tholan.'

The Hawkinsite groped for it eagerly. His supple fingers manipulated the hose and the needle valve with the utmost delicacy. In the space of ten seconds, he had it in place and was inhaling the gas in huge breaths. His eyes were growing clear and transparent.

Drake waited until the Hawkinsite's breathing had subsided to normal, and then, without expression, he raised his needle-gun and fired. Rose screamed. The Hawkinsite remained standing. His four lower limbs were incapable of buckling, but his head lolled and from his suddenly flaccid mouth, the cyanide hose fell, disregarded. Once again, Drake closed the needle valve and now he tossed the cylinder aside and stood there somberly, looking at the dead creature. There was no external mark to show that he had been killed. The needle-gun's pellet, thinner than the needle which gave the gun its name, entered the body noiselessly and easily, and exploded with devastating effect only within the abdominal cavity.

Rose ran from the room, still screaming. Drake pursued her, seized her arm. She heard the hard, flat sounds of his palm against her face without feeling them and subsided into little bubbling sobs.

Drake said, 'I told you to have nothing to do with this. Now what do you think you'll do?'

She said, 'Let me go. I want to leave. I want to go away.'

'Because of something it was my job to do? You heard what the creature was saying. Do you suppose I could allow him to return to his world and spread those lies? They would believe him. And what do you think would happen then? Can you imagine what an interstellar war might be like? They would imagine they would have to kill us all to stop the disease.'

With an effort that seemed to turn her inside out, Rose steadied. She looked firmly into Drake's eyes and said, 'What Dr. Tholan said were no lies and no mistakes, Drake.'

'Oh, come now, you're hysterical. You need sleep.'

'I know what he said is so because the Security Commission knows all about that same theory, and knows it to be true.'

'Why do you say such a preposterous thing?'

'Because you yourself let that slip twice.'

Drake said, 'Sit down.' She did so, and he stood there, looking curiously at her. 'So I have given myself away twice, have I? You've had a busy day of detection, my dear. You have facets you keep well hidden.' He sat down and crossed his legs.

Rose thought, yes, she had had a busy day. She could see the electric clock on the kitchen wall from where she sat; it was more than two hours past midnight. Harg Tholan had entered their house thirty-five hours before and now he lay murdered in the spare bedroom.

Drake said, 'Well, aren't you going to tell me where I pulled my two boners?'

'You turned white when Harg Tholan referred to me as a charming hostess. Hostess has a double meaning, you know, Drake. A host is one who harbors a parasite.'

'Number one,' said Drake. 'What's number two?'

'That's something you did before Harg Tholan entered the house. I've been trying to remember it for hours. Do *you* remember, Drake? You spoke about how unpleasant it was for Hawkinsites to associate with Earthmen, and I said Harg Tholan was a doctor and had to. I asked you if you thought that human doctors particularly enjoyed going to the tropics, or letting infected mosquitoes bite them. Do you remember how upset you became?'

Drake laughed. 'I had no idea I was so transparent. Mosquitoes are hosts for the malaria and yellow-fever parasites.' He sighed. 'I've done my best to keep you out of this. I tried to keep the Hawkinsite away. I tried threatening you. Now there's nothing left but to tell you the truth. I must, because only the truth – or death – will keep you quiet. And I don't want to kill you.'

She shrank back in her chair, eyes wide.

Drake said, 'The Commission knows the truth. It does us no good. We can only do all in our power to prevent the other world from finding out.'

'But the truth can't be held down forever! Harg Tholan found out. You've killed him, but another extraterrestrial will repeat the same discovery – over and over again. You can't kill them all.'

'We know that, too,' agreed Drake. 'We have no choice.'

'Why?' cried Rose. 'Harg Tholan gave you the solution. He made no suggestions or threats of war between worlds. He suggested that we combine with the other intelligences and help to wipe out the parasite. And we can! If we, in common with all the others, put every scrap of effort into it –'

'You mean we can trust him? Does he speak for his government or for the other races?'

'Can we dare to refuse the risk?'

Drake said, 'You don't understand.' He reached toward her and took one of her cold, unresisting hands between both of his. He went on, 'I may seem silly trying to teach you anything about your speciality, but I want you to hear me out. Harg Tholan was right. Man and his prehistoric ancestors have been living with this parasitic intelligence for uncounted ages; certainly for a much longer period than we have been truly *Homo sapiens*. In that interval, we have not only become adapted to it, we have become dependent upon it. It is no longer a case of parasitism. It is a case of mutual cooperation. You biologists have a name for it.'

She tore her hand away. 'What are you talking about? Symbiosis?'

'Exactly. We have a disease of our own, remember. It is a reverse disease; one of unrestrained growth. We've mentioned it already as a contrast to the Inhibition Death. Well, what is the cause of cancer? How long have biologists, physiologists, biochemists and all the others been working on it? How much success have they had with it? Why? Can't you answer that for yourself now?'

She said slowly, 'No, I can't. What are you talking about?'

'It's all very well to say that if we could remove the parasite, we would have eternal growth and life if we wanted it; or at least until we got tired of being too big or of living too long, and did away with ourselves neatly. But how many millions of years has it been since the human body has had occasion to grow in such an unrestrained fashion? Can it do so any longer? Is the chemistry of the body adjusted to that? Has it got the proper whatchamacallits?'

'Enzymes,' Rose supplied in a whisper.

'Yes, enzymes. It's impossible for us. If for any reason the parasitic intelligence, as Harg Tholan calls it, does leave the human body, or if its relationship to the human mind is in any way impaired, growth does take place, but not in any orderly fashion. We call the growth cancer. And there you have it. There's no way of getting rid of the parasite. We're together for all eternity. To get rid of their Inhibition Death, extraterrestrials must first wipe out all vertebrate life on Earth. There is no other solution for them, and so we must keep knowledge of it from them. Do you understand?'

Her mouth was dry and it was difficult to talk. 'I understand, Drake.' She noticed that his forehead was damp and that there was a line of perspiration down each cheek. 'And now you'll have to get it out of the apartment.'

'It's late at night and I'll be able to get the body out of the building. From there on –' He turned to her. 'I don't know when I'll be back.'

'I understand, Drake,' she said again.

Harg Tholan was heavy. Drake had to drag him through the apartment. Rose turned away, retching. She hid her eyes until she heard the front door close. She whispered to herself, 'I understand, Drake.'

It was 3 a.m. Nearly an hour had passed since she heard the front door click gently into place behind Drake and his burden. She didn't know where he was going, what he intended doing –

She sat there numbly. There was no desire to sleep; no desire to move. She kept her mind traveling in tight circles, away from the thing she knew and which she wanted not to know.

Parasitic minds! Was it only a coincidence or was it some queer racial memory, some tenuous long-sustained wisp of tradition or insight, stretching back through incredible millennia, that kept current the odd myth of human beginnings? She thought to herself, there were two inelligences on Earth to begin with. There were humans in the Garden of Eden and also the serpent, which 'was more subtil than any beast of the field'. The serpent infected man and, as a result, it lost its limbs. Its physical attributes were no longer necessary. And because of the infection, man was driven out of the Garden of eternal life. Death entered the world.

Yet, despite her efforts, the circle of her thoughts expanded and returned to Drake. She shoved and it returned; she counted to herself, she recited the names of the objects in her field of vision, she cried, 'No, no, no,' and it returned. It kept returning.

Drake had lied to her. It had been a plausible story. It would have held good under most circumstances; but Drake was not a biologist. Cancer could not be, as Drake had said, a disease that was an expression of a lost ability for normal growth. Cancer attacked children while they were still growing; it could even attack embryonic tissue. It attacked fish, which, like extraterrestrials, never stopped growing while they lived, and died only by disease or accident. It attacked plants which had no minds and could not be parasitized. Cancer had nothing to do with the presence or absence of normal growth; it was the general disease of life, to which *no* tissue of *no* multicellular organism was completely immune.

He should not have bothered lying. He should not have allowed some obscure sentimental weakness to persuade him to avoid the necessity of killing her in that manner. She would tell them at the Institute. The parasite *could* be beaten. Its absence would *not* cause cancer. But who would believe her?

She put her hands over her eyes. The young men who disappeared were usually in the first year of their marriage. Whatever the process of reproduction of the parasite intelligences, it must involve close association with another parasite – the type of close and continuous association that might only be possible if their respective hosts were in equally close relationship. As in the case of newly married couples.

She could feel her thoughts slowly disconnect. They would be coming to her. They would be saying, 'Where is Harg Tholan?' And she would answer, 'With my husband.' Only they would say, 'Where is your husband?' because he would be gone, too. He needed her no longer. He would never return. They would never find him, because he would be out in space. She would report them both, Drake Smollett and Harg Tholan, to the Missing Persons Bureau.

She wanted to weep, but couldn't; she was dry-eyed and it was painful.

And then she began to giggle and couldn't stop. It was very funny. She had looked for the answers to so many questions and had found them all. She had even found the answer to the questions she thought had no bearing on the subject.

She had finally learned why Drake had married her.

The dropping of the atomic bomb in 1945 made science fiction respectable. Once the horror at Hiroshima took place, anyone could see that science fiction writers were not merely dreamers and crackpots after all, and that many of the motifs of that class of literature were now permanently part of the newspaper headlines.

I suppose that science fiction writers and readers were, on the whole, pleased – if not at the effect of the atom bomb itself, then at least at the crystallization into fact of something that had been so science fictional.

I myself was ambivalent. Quite apart from the frightening aspects of nuclear explosions and the mildly irrational feeling that such things as atom bombs belonged to us and not to the real world, I also felt that reality might have a stultifying effect on the field.

And I think it did to a certain extent. There was a tendency for the new reality to nail the science fiction writer to the ground. Prior to 1945, science fiction had been wild and free. All its motifs and plot varieties remained in the realm of fantasy and we could do as we pleased. After 1945, there came the increasing need to talk about the A.E.C and to mold all the infinite scope of our thoughts to the small bit of them that had become real.

In fact, there was the birth of something I called 'tomorrow fiction': the science fiction story that was no more new than tomorrow's headlines.

Believe me, there can be nothing duller than tomorrow's headlines in science fiction. As an example, consider Nevil Shute's On the Beach. *Surely to the science fiction fan – as opposed to the general public – this must seem very milk-and-watery. So there's a nuclear war to start the story with – and what else is new?*

I resisted the temptation to base a story slavishly on the present until I could think of a way to do so without making myself a minion of the headlines and of topicality. I wanted to write a story that would deal with the things of tomorrow without becoming outdated the day after tomorrow.

The result was 'Breeds There a Man . . .?' which, despite all its topicality, is as much science fiction now as it was in 1951 when it was written.

First appearance – Astounding Science Fiction, June 1951. Copyright, 1951, by Street & Smith Publications, Inc.

Police Sergeant Mankiewicz was on the telephone and he wasn't enjoying it. His conversation was sounding like a one-sided view of a firecracker.

He was saying, 'That's right! He came in here and said, "Put me in jail, because I want to kill myself."

'. . . I can't help that. Those were his exact words. It sounds crazy to me, too.

'. . . Look, mister, the guy answers the description. You asked me for information and I'm giving it to you.

'. . . He has exactly that scar on his right cheek and he said his name was John Smith. He didn't say it was Doctor anything-at-all.

'. . . Well, sure it's a phony. Nobody is named John Smith. Not in a police station, anyway.

'. . . He's in jail now.

'. . . Yes, I mean it.

'. . . Resisting an officer; assault and battery; malicious mischief. That's three counts.

'. . . I don't care who he is.

'. . . All right. I'll hold on.'

He looked up at Officer Brown and put his hand over the mouthpiece of the phone. It was a ham of a hand that nearly swallowed up the phone altogether. His blunt-featured face was ruddy and steaming under a thatch of pale-yellow hair.

He said, 'Trouble! Nothing but trouble at a precinct station. I'd rather be pounding a beat any day.'

'Who's on the phone?' asked Brown. He had just come in and didn't really care. He thought Mankiewicz would look better on a suburban beat, too.

'Oak Ridge. Long Distance. A guy called Grant. Head of somethingological division, and now he's getting somebody else at seventy-five cents a min . . . Hello!'

Mankiewicz got a new grip on the phone and held himself down.

'Look,' he said, 'let me go through this from the beginning. I want you to get it straight and then if you don't like it, you can send someone down here. The guy doesn't want a lawyer. He claims he just wants to stay in jail and, brother, that's all right with me.

'Well, will you listen? He came in yesterday, walked right up to me, and said, "Officer, I want you to put me in jail because I want to kill myself." So I said, "Mister, I'm sorry you want to kill yourself. Don't do it, because if you do, you'll regret it the rest of your life."

'. . . I *am* serious. I'm just telling you what I said. I'm not saying it was a funny joke, but I've got my own troubles here, if you know what I mean. Do you think all I've got to do here is to listen to cranks who walk in and —

' ". . . Give me a chance, will you?" I said, "I can't put you in jail for wanting to kill yourself. That's no crime." And he said, "But I don't want to die." So I said, "Look, bud, get out of here." I mean if a guy wants to commit suicide, all right, and if he doesn't want to, all right, but I don't want him weeping on my shoulder.

'. . . I'm *getting* on with it. So he said to me, "If I commit a crime, will you put me in jail?" I said, "If you're caught and if someone files a charge and you can't put up bail, we will. Now beat it." So he picked up the inkwell on my desk and, before I could stop him, he turned it upside down on the open police blotter.

'. . . That's right! Why do you think we have "malicious mischief" tabbed on him? The ink ran down all over my pants.

'. . . Yes, assault and battery, too! I came hopping down to shake a little sense into him, and he kicked me in the shins and handed me one in the eye.

'. . . I'm not making this up. You want to come down here and look at my face?

'. . . He'll be up in court one of these days. About Thursday, maybe.

'. . . Ninety days is the least he'll get, unless the psychoes say otherwise. I think he belongs in the loony-bin myself.

'. . . Officially, he's John Smith. That's the only name he'll give.

'. . . No, sir, he doesn't get released without the proper legal steps.

'. . . O.K., you do that, if you want to, bud! I just do my job here.'

He barged the phone into its cradle, glowered at it, then picked it up and began dialing. He said 'Gianetti?', got the proper answer and began talking.

'What's the A.E.C.? I've been talking to some Joe on the phone and he says –

'... No, I'm not kidding, lunk-head. If I were kidding, I'd put up a sign. What's the alphabet soup?'

He listened, said, 'Thanks' in a small voice and hung up again.

He had lost some of his color. 'That second guy was the head of the Atomic Energy Commission,' he said to Brown. 'They must have switched me from Oak Ridge to Washington.'

Brown lounged to his feet, 'Maybe the F.B.I. is after this John Smith guy. Maybe he's one of these here scientists.' He felt moved to philosophy. 'They ought to keep atomic secrets away from those guys. Things were O.K. as long as General Groves was the only fella who knew about the atom bomb. Once they cut in these here scientists on it, though –'

'Ah, shut up,' snarled Mankiewicz.

Dr. Oswald Grant kept his eyes fixed on the white line that marked the highway and handled the car as though it were an enemy of his. He always did. He was tall and knobby with a withdrawn expression stamped on his face. His knees crowded the wheel, and his knuckles whitened whenever he made a turn.

Inspector Darrity sat beside him with his legs crossed so that the sole of his left shoe came up hard against the door. It would leave a sandy mark when he took it away. He tossed a nut-brown penknife from hand to hand. Earlier, he had unsheathed its wicked, gleaming blade and scraped casually at his nails as they drove, but a sudden swerve had nearly cost him a finger and he desisted.

He said, 'What do you know about this Ralson?'

Dr. Grant took his eyes from the road momentarily, then returned them. He said, uneasily, 'I've known him since he took his doctorate at Princeton. He's a very brilliant man.'

'Yes? Brilliant, huh? Why is it that all you scientific men describe one another as "brilliant"? Aren't there any mediocre ones?'

'Many. I'm one of them. But Ralston isn't. You ask anyone. Ask Oppenheimer. Ask Bush. He was the youngest observer at Alamogordo.'

'O.K. He was brilliant. What about his private life?'

Grant waited. 'I wouldn't know.'

'You know him since Princeton. How many years is that?'

They had been scouring north along the highway from Washington for two hours with scarcely a word between them. Now Grant felt the atmosphere change and the grip of the law on his coat collar.

'He got his degree in '43.'

'You've known him eight years then.'

'That's right.'

'And you don't know about his private life?'

'A man's life is his own, Inspector. He wasn't very sociable. A great many of the men are like that. They work under pressure and when they're off the job, they're not interested in continuing the lab acquaintanceships.'

'Did he belong to any organization that you know of?'

'No.'

The inspector said, 'Did he ever say anything to you that might indicate he was disloyal?'

Grant shouted 'No!' and there was silence for a while.

Then Darrity said, 'How important is Ralson in atomic research?'

Grant hunched over the wheel and said, 'As important as any one man can be. I grant you that no one is indispensable, but Ralson has always seemed to be rather unique. He has the engineering mentality.'

'What does that mean?'

'He isn't much of a mathematician himself, but he can work out the gadgets that put someone else's math into life. There's no one like him when it comes to that. Time and again, Inspector, we've had a problem to lick and no time to lick it. There were nothing but blank minds all around until he put some thought into it and said, "Why don't you try so-and-so?" Then he'd go away. He wouldn't even be interested enough to see if it worked. But it always did. Always! Maybe we would have got it ourselves eventually, but it might have taken months of additional time. I don't know how he does it. It's no use asking him either. He just looks at you and says "It was obvious", and walks away. Of course, once he's shown us how to do it, it *is* obvious.'

The inspector let him have his say out. When no more came, he said, 'Would you say he was queer, mentally? Erratic, you know.'

'When a person is a genius, you wouldn't expect him to be normal, would you?'

'Maybe not. But just how abnormal was this particular genius?'

'He never talked, particularly. Sometimes, he wouldn't work.'

'Stayed at home and went fishing instead?'

'No. He came to the labs all right; but he would just sit at his desk. Sometimes that would go on for weeks. Wouldn't answer you, or even look at you, when you spoke to him.'

'Did he ever actually leave work altogether?'

'Before now, you mean? Never!'

'Did he ever claim he wanted to commit suicide? Ever say he wouldn't feel safe except in jail?'

'No.'

'You're sure this John Smith is Ralson?'

'I'm almost positive. He has a chemical burn on his right cheek that can't be mistaken.'

'O.K. That's that, then I'll speak to him and see what he sounds like.'

The silence fell for good this time. Dr. Grant followed the snaking line as Inspector Darrity tossed the penknife in low arcs from hand to hand.

The warden listened to the call-box and looked up at his visitors. 'We can have him brought up here, Inspector, regardless.'

'No,' Dr. Grant shook his head. 'Let's go to him.'

Darrity said, 'Is that normal for Ralson, Dr. Grant? Would you expect him to attack a guard trying to take him out of a prison cell?'

Grant said, 'I can't say.'

The warden spread a calloused palm. His thick nose twitched a little. 'We haven't tried to do anything about him so far because of the telegram from Washington, but, frankly, he doesn't belong here. I'll be glad to have him taken off my hands.'

'We'll see him in his cell,' said Darrity.

They went down the hard, barlined corridor. Empty, incurious eyes watched their passing.

Dr. Grant felt his flesh crawl. 'Has he been kept *here* all the time?'

Darrity did not answer.

The guard, pacing before them, stopped. 'This is the cell.'

Darrity said, 'Is that Dr. Ralson?'

Dr. Grant looked silently at the figure upon the cot. The man had been lying down when they first reached the cell, but now he had risen to one elbow and seemed to be trying to shrink into the wall. His hair was sandy and thin, his figure slight, his eyes blank and china-blue. On his right cheek there was a raised pink patch that tailed off like a tadpole.

Dr. Grant said, 'That's Ralson.'

The guard opened the door and stepped inside, but Inspector Darrity sent him out again with a gesture. Ralson watched them mutely. He had drawn both feet up to the cot and was pushing backwards. His Adam's apple bobbled as he swallowed.

Darrity said quietly, 'Dr. Elwood Ralson?'

'What do you want?' The voice was a surprising baritone.

'Would you come with us, please? We have some questions we would like to ask you.'

'No! Leave me alone!'

'Dr. Ralson,' said Grant, 'I've been sent here to ask you to come back to work.'

Ralson looked at the scientist and there was a momentary glint of something other than fear in his eyes. He said, 'Hello, Grant.' He got off his cot. 'Listen, I've been trying to have them put me into a padded cell. Can't you make them do that for me? You know me, Grant. I wouldn't ask for something I didn't feel was necessary. Help me. I can't stand the hard walls. It makes me want to . . . bash –' He brought the flat of his palm thudding down against the hard, dull-gray concrete behind his cot.

Darrity looked thoughtful. He brought out his penknife and unbent the gleaming blade. Carefully, he scraped at his thumbnail, and said, 'Would you like to see a doctor?'

But Ralson didn't answer that. He followed the gleam of metal and his lips parted and grew wet. His breath became ragged and harsh.

He said, 'Put that away!'

Darrity paused. 'Put what away?'

'The knife. Don't hold it in front of me. I can't stand looking at it.'

Darrity said, 'Why not?' He held it out. 'Anything wrong with it? It's a good knife.'

Ralson lunged. Darrity stepped back and his left hand came

down on the other's wrist. He lifted the knife high in the air. 'What's the matter, Ralson? What are you after?'

Grant cried a protest but Darrity waved him away.

Darrity said, 'What do you want, Ralson?'

Ralson tried to reach upward, and bent under the other's appalling grip. He gasped, 'Give me the knife.'

'Why, Ralson? What do you want to do with it?'

'Please. I've got to –' He was pleading. 'I've got to stop living.'

'You want to die?'

'No. But I must.'

Darrity shoved. Ralson flailed backward and tumbled into his cot, so that it squeaked noisily. Slowly, Darrity bent the blade of his penknife into its sheath and put it away. Ralson covered his face. His shoulders were shaking but otherwise he did not move.

There was the sound of shouting from the corridor, as the other prisoners reacted to the noise issuing from Ralson's cell. The guard came hurrying down, yelling, 'Quiet!' as he went.

Darrity looked up. 'It's all right, guard.'

He was wiping his hands upon a large white handkerchief. 'I think we'll get a doctor for him.'

Dr. Gottfried Blaustein was small and dark and spoke with a trace of an Austrian accent. He needed only a small goatee to be the layman's caricature of a psychiatrist. But he was clean-shaven, and very carefully dressed. He watched Grant closely, assessing him, blocking in certain observations and deductions. He did this automatically, now, with everyone he met.

He said, 'You give me a sort of picture. You describe a man of great talent, perhaps even genius. You tell me he has always been uncomfortable with people; that he has never fitted in with his laboratory environment, even though it was there that he met the greatest of success. Is there another environment to which he has fitted himself?'

'I don't understand.'

'It is not given to all of us to be so fortunate as to find a congenial type of company at the place or in the field where we find it necessary to make a living. Often, one compensates by playing an instrument, or going hiking, or joining some club. In other words, one creates a new type of society, when not working, in which one can feel more at home. It need not have the slightest connection with what one's ordinary occupation is. It is an escape, and not necessarily an unhealthy one.' He smiled and added, 'Myself, I collect stamps. I am an active member of the American Society of Philatelists.'

Grant shook his head. 'I don't know what he did outside working hours. I doubt that he did anything like what you've mentioned.'

'Um-m-m. Well, that would be sad. Relaxation and enjoyment are wherever you find them; but you must find them somewhere, no?'

'Have you spoken to Dr. Ralson yet?'

'About his problems? No.'

'Aren't you going to?'

'Oh, yes. But he has been here only a week. One must give him a chance to recover. He was in a highly excited state when he first came here. It was almost a delirium. Let him rest and become accustomed to the new environment. I will question him, then.'

'Will you be able to get him back to work?'

Blaustein smiled. 'How should I know? I don't even know what his sickness is.'

'Couldn't you at least get rid of the worst of it, this suicidal obsession of his, and take care of the rest of the cure while he's at work?'

'Perhaps. I couldn't even venture an opinion so far without several interviews.'

'How long do you suppose it will all take?'

'In these matters, Dr. Grant, nobody can say.'

Grant brought his hands together in a sharp slap. 'Do what seems best then. But this is more important than you know.'

'Perhaps. But you may be able to help me, Dr. Grant.'

'How?'

'Can you get me certain information which may be classified as top secret?'

'What kind of information?'

'I would like to know the suicide rate, since 1945, among nuclear scientists. Also, how many have left their jobs to go into other types of scientific work, or to leave science altogether.'

'Is this in connection with Ralson?'

'Don't you think it might be an occupational disease, this terrible unhappiness of his?'

'Well – a good many have left their jobs, naturally.'

'Why naturally, Dr. Grant?'

'You must know how it is, Dr. Blaustein. The atmosphere in modern atomic research is one of great pressure and red tape. You work with the government; you work with military men. You can't talk about your work; you have to be careful what you say. Naturally, if you get a chance at a job in a university, where you can fix your own hours, do your own work, write papers that don't have to be submitted to the A.E.C., attend conventions that aren't held behind locked doors, you take it.'

'And abandon your field of speciality forever.'

'There are always non-military applications. Of course, there was one man who did leave for another reason. He told me once he couldn't sleep nights. He said he'd hear one hundred thousand screams coming from Hiroshima, when he put the lights out. The last I heard of him he was a clerk in a haberdashery.'

'And do you ever hear a few screams yourself?'

Grant nodded. 'It isn't a nice feeling to know that even a little of the responsibility of atomic destruction might be your own.'

'How did Ralson feel?'

'He never spoke of anything like that.'

'In other words, if he felt like it, he never even had the safety-valve effect of letting off steam to the rest of you.'

'I guess he hadn't.'

'Yet nuclear research must be done, no?'

'I'll say.'

'What would you do, Dr. Grant, if you felt you *had* to do something that you *couldn't* do.'

Grant shrugged. 'I don't know.'

'Some people kill themselves.'

'You mean that's what has Ralson down.'

'I don't know. I do not know. I will speak to Dr. Ralson this evening. I can promise nothing, of course, but I will let you know whatever I can.'

Grant rose. 'Thanks, Doctor. I'll try to get the information you want.'

Elwood Ralson's appearance had improved in the week he had been at Dr. Blaustein's sanatorium. His face had filled out and some of the restlessness had gone out of him. He was tieless and beltless. His shoes were without laces.

Blaustein said, 'How do you feel, Dr. Ralson?'

'Rested.'

'You have been treated well?'

'No complaints, Doctor.'

Blaustein's hand fumbled for the letter-opener with which it was his habit to play during moments of abstraction, but his fingers met nothing. It had been put away, of course, with anything else possessing a sharp edge. There was nothing on his desk, now, but papers.

He said, 'Sit down, Dr. Ralson. How do your symptoms progress?'

'You mean, do I have what you would call a suicidal impulse? Yes. It gets worse or better, depending on my thoughts, I think. But it's always with me. There is nothing you can do to help.'

'Perhaps you are right. There are often things I cannot help. But I would like to know as much as I can about you. You are an important man —'

Ralson snorted.

'You do not consider that to be so?' asked Blaustein.

'No, I don't. There are no important men, any more than there are important individual bacteria.'

'I don't understand.'

'I don't expect you to.'

'And yet it seems to me that behind your statement there must have been much thought. It would certainly be of the greatest interest to have you tell me some of this thought.'

For the first time, Ralson smiled. It was not a pleasant smile. His nostrils were white. He said, 'It is amusing to watch you, Doctor. You go about your business so conscientiously. You must listen to me, mustn't you, with just that air of phony interest and unctuous sympathy. I can tell you the most ridiculous things and still be sure of an audience, can't I?'

'Don't you think my interest can be real, even granted that it is professional, too?'

'No, I don't.'

'Why not?'

'I'm not interested in discussing it.'

'Would you rather return to your room?'

'If you don't mind. No!' His voice had suddenly suffused with fury as he stood up, then almost immediately sat down again. 'Why shouldn't I use you? I don't like to talk to people. They're stupid. They don't see things. They stare at the obvious for hours and it means nothing to them. If I spoke to them, they wouldn't understand; they'd lose patience; they'd laugh. Whereas you must listen. It's your job. You can't interrupt to tell me I'm mad, even though you may think so.'

'I'd be glad to listen to whatever you would like to tell me.'

Ralson drew a deep breath. 'I've known something for a year now, that very few people know. Maybe it's something no *live* person knows. Do you know that human cultural advances come in spurts? Over a space of two generations in a city containing thirty thousand free men, enough literary and artistic genius of the first rank arose to supply a nation of millions for a century under ordinary circumstances. I'm referring to the Athens of Pericles.

'There are other examples. There is the Florence of the Medicis, the England of Elizabeth, the Spain of the Cordovan Emirs. There was the spasm of social reformers among the Israelites of the Eighth and Seventh centuries before Christ. Do you know what I mean?'

Blaustein nodded. 'I see that history is a subject that interests you.'

'Why not? I suppose there's nothing that says I must restrict myself to nuclear cross-sections and wave mechanics.'

'Nothing at all. Please proceed.'

'At first, I thought I could learn more of the true inwardness of historical cycles by consulting a specialist. I had some conferences with a professional historian. A waste of time!'

'What was his name; this professional historian?'

'Does it matter?'

'Perhaps not, if you would rather consider it confidential. What did he tell you?'

'He said I was wrong: that history only appeared to go in spasms. He said that after closer studies the great civilizations of Egypt and Sumeria did not arise suddenly or out of nothing, but upon the basis of a long-developing sub-civilization that was already sophisticated in its arts. He said that Periclean Athens built upon a pre-Periclean Athens of lower accomplishments, without which the age of Pericles could not have been.

'I asked why was there not a post-Periclean Athens of higher accomplishments still, and he told me that Athens was ruined by a plague and by a long war with Sparta. I asked about other cultural spurts and each time it was a war that ended it, or, in some cases, even accompanied it. He was like all the rest. The truth was there; he had only to bend and pick it up; but he didn't.'

Ralson stared at the floor, and said in a tired voice, 'They come to me in the laboratory sometimes, Doctor. They say, "How the devil are we going to get rid of the such-and-such effect that is ruining all our measurements, Ralson?" They show me the instruments and the wiring diagrams and I say, "It's staring at you. Why don't you do so-and-so? A child could tell you that." Then I walk away because I can't endure the slow puzzling of their stupid faces. Later, they come to me and say, "It worked, Ralson. How did you figure it out?" I can't explain to them, Doctor; it would be like explaining that water is wet. And I couldn't explain to the historian. And I can't explain to you. It's a waste of time.'

'Would you like to go back to your room?'

'Yes.'

Blaustein sat and wondered for many minutes after Ralson had been escorted out of his office. His fingers found their way automatically into the upper right drawer of his desk and lifted out the letter-opener. He twiddled it in his fingers.

Finally, he lifted the telephone and dialed the unlisted number he had been given.

He said, 'This is Blaustein. There is a professional historian who was consulted by Dr. Ralson some time in the past, probably a bit over a year ago. I don't know his name. I don't even know if he was connected with a university. If you could find him, I would like to see him.'

Thaddeus Milton, Ph.D., blinked thoughtfully at Blaustein and brushed his hand through his iron-gray hair. He said, 'They came to me and I said that I had indeed met this man. However, I have had very little connection with him. None, in fact, beyond a few conversations of a professional nature.'

'How did he come to you?'

'He wrote me a letter; why me, rather than someone else, I do not know. A series of articles written by myself had appeared in one of the semi-learned journals of semi-popular appeal about that time. It may have attracted his attention.'

'I see. With what general topic were the articles concerned?'

'They were a consideration of the validity of the cyclic approach to history. That is, whether one can really say that a particular civilization must follow laws of growth and decline in any matter analogous to those involving individuals.'

'I have read Toynbee, Dr. Milton.'

'Well, then, you know what I mean.'

Blaustein said, 'And when Dr. Ralson consulted you, was it with reference to this cyclic approach to history?'

'Um-m-m. In a way, I suppose. Of course, the man is not an historian and some of his notions about cultural trends are rather dramatic and ... what shall I say ... tabloidish. Pardon me, Doctor, if I ask a question which may be improper. Is Dr. Ralson one of your patients?'

'Dr. Ralson is not well and is in my care. This, and all else we say here, is confidential, of course.'

'Quite. I understand that. However, your answer explains something to me. Some of his ideas almost verged on the irrational. He was always worried, it seemed to me, about the connection between what he called "cultural spurts" and calamities of one sort or another. Now such connections have been noted frequently. The time of a nation's greatest vitality may come at a time of great national insecurity. The Netherlands is a good case in point. Her great artists, statesmen, and explorers belong to the early seventeenth century at a time when she was locked in a death struggle with the greatest European power of the time, Spain. When at the point of destruction at home, she was building an empire in the Far East and had secured footholds on the northern coast of South America, the southern tip of Africa, and the Hudson Valley of North America. Her fleets fought England to a standstill. And then, once her political safety was assured, she declined.

'Well, as I say, that is not unusual. Groups, like individuals, will rise to strange heights in answer to a challenge, and vegetate in the absence of a challenge. Where Dr. Ralson left the paths of sanity, however, was in insisting that such a view amounted to confusing cause and effect. He declared that it was not times of war and danger that stimulated "cultural spurts", but rather vice versa. He claimed that each time a group of men showed too much vitality and ability, a war became necessary to destroy the possibility of their further development.'

'I see,' said Blaustein.

'I rather laughed at him, I am afraid. It may be that that was why he did not keep the last appointment we made. Just toward the end of that last conference he asked me, in the most intense fashion imaginable, whether I did not think it queer that such an improbable species as man was dominant on earth, when all he had in his favor was intelligence. There I laughed aloud. Perhaps I should not have, poor fellow.'

'It was a natural reaction,' said Blaustein, 'But I must take no more of your time. You have been most helpful.'

They shook hands, and Thaddeus Milton took his leave.

'Well,' said Darrity, 'there are your figures on the recent suicides among scientific personnel. Get any deductions out of it?'

'I should be asking you that,' said Blaustein, gently. 'The F.B.I. must have investigated thoroughly.'

'You can bet the national debt on that. They *are* suicides. There's no mistake about it. There have been people checking on it in another department. The rate is about four times above normal, taking age, social status, economic class into consideration.'

'What about British scientists?'

'Just about the same.'

'And the Soviet Union?'

'Who can tell?' The investigator leaned forward. 'Doc, you don't think the Soviets have some sort of ray that can make people want to commit suicide, do you? It's sort of suspicious that men in atomic research are the only ones affected.'

'Is it? Perhaps not. Nuclear physicists may have peculiar strains imposed upon them. It is difficult to tell without thorough study.'

'You mean complexes might be coming through?' asked Darrity, warily.

Blaustein made a face. 'Psychiatry is becoming too popular. Everybody talks of complexes and neuroses and psychoses and compulsions and what-not. One man's guilt complex is another man's good night's sleep. If I could talk to one of the men who committed suicide, maybe I could know something.'

'You're talking to Ralson.'

'Yes, I'm talking to Ralson.'

'Has *he* got a guilt complex?'

'Not particularly. He has a background out of which it would not surprise me if he obtained a morbid concern with death. When he was twelve he saw his mother die under the wheels of an automobile. His father died slowly of cancer. Yet the effect of those experiences on his present troubles is not clear.'

Darrity picked up his hat. 'Well, I wish you'd get a move on, Doc. There's something big on, bigger than the H-Bomb. I don't know how anything *can* be bigger than that, but it is.'

Ralson insisted on standing. 'I had a bad night last night, Doctor.'

'I hope', said Blaustein, 'these conferences are not disturbing you.'

'Well, maybe they are. They have me thinking on the subject again. It makes things bad, when I do that. How do you imagine it feels being part of a bacterial culture, Doctor?'

'I had never thought of that. To a bacterium, it probably feels quite normal.'

Ralson did not hear. He said, slowly. 'A culture in which intelligence is being studied. We study all sorts of things as far as their genetic relationships are concerned. We take fruit flies and cross red eyes and white eyes to see what happens. We don't care anything about red eyes and white eyes, but we try to gather from them certain basic genetic principles. You see what I mean?'

'Certainly.'

'Even in humans, we can follow various physical characteristics. There are the Hapsburg lips, and the haemophilia that started with Queen Victoria and cropped up in her descendants among the Spanish and Russian royal families. We can even follow feeble-mindedness in the Jukeses and Kallikaks. You learn about it in high-school biology. But you can't breed human beings the way you do fruit flies. Humans live too long. It would take centuries to draw conclusions. It's a pity we don't have a special race of men that reproduce at weekly intervals, eh?'

He waited for an answer, but Blaustein only smiled.

Ralston said, 'Only that's exactly what we would be for another group of beings whose life span might be thousands of years. To them, we would reproduce rapidly enough. We would be short-lived creatures and they could study the genetics of such things as musical aptitude, scientific intelligence, and so on. Not that those things would interest them as such, any more than the white eyes of the fruit fly interest us as white eyes.'

'This is a very interesting notion,' said Blaustein.

'It is not simply a notion. It is true. To me, it is obvious, and I don't care how it seems to you. Look around you. Look at the planet, Earth. What kind of a ridiculous animal are we to be lords of the world after the dinosaurs had failed? Sure, we're intelligent, but what's intelligence? We think it is important because we have it. If the Tyranosaurus could have picked out the one quality that he thought would ensure species domination, it would be size and strength. And he would make a better case for it. He lasted longer than we're likely to.

'Intelligence in itself isn't much as far as survival values are concerned. The elephant makes out very poorly indeed when compared to the sparrow even though he is much more intelligent. The dog does well, under man's protection, but not as well as the housefly against whom every human hand is raised. Or take the primates as a group. The small ones cower before their enemies; the large ones have always been remarkably unsuccessful in doing more than barely holding their own. The baboons do the best and that is because of their canines, not their brains.'

A light film of perspiration covered Ralson's forehead. 'And one can see that man has been tailored, made to careful specifications for those things that study us. Generally, the primate is short-lived. Naturally, the larger ones live longer, which is a fairly general rule in animal life. Yet the human being has a life span twice as long as any of the other great apes; considerably longer even than the gorilla that outweighs him. We mature later. It's as though we've been carefully bred to live a little longer so that our life cycle might be of a more convenient length.'

He jumped to his feet, shaking his fists above his head. 'A thousand years are but as yesterday –'

Blaustein punched a button hastily.

For a moment, Ralson struggled against the white-coated orderly who entered, and then he allowed himself to be led away.

Blaustein looked after him, shook his head, and picked up the telephone.

He got Darrity. 'Inspector, you may as well know that this may take a long time.'

He listened and shook his head. 'I know. I don't minimize the urgency.'

The voice in the receiver was tinny and harsh. 'Doctor, you

are minimizing it. I'll send Dr. Grant to you. He'll explain the situation to you.'

Dr. Grant asked how Ralson was, then asked somewhat wistfully if he could see him. Blaustein shook his head gently.

Grant said, 'I've been directed to explain the current situation in atomic research to you.'

'So that I will understand, no?'

'I hope so. It's a measure of desperation. I'll have to remind you –'

'Not to breathe a word of it. Yes, I know. This insecurity on the part of you people is a very bad symptom. You must know these things cannot be hidden.'

'You live with secrecy. It's contagious.'

'Exactly. What is the current secret?'

'There is . . . or, at least, there might be a defense against the atomic bomb.'

'And that is a secret? It would be better if it were shouted to all the people of the world instantly.'

'For heaven's sake, no. Listen to me, Dr. Blaustein. It's only on paper so far. It's at the E equal mc square stage, almost. It may not be practical. It would be bad to raise hopes we would have to disappoint. On the other hand, if it were known that we *almost* had a defense, there *might* be a desire to start and win a war before the defense were completely developed.'

'That I don't believe. But, nevertheless, I distract you. What is the nature of this defense, or have you told me as much as you dare?'

'No, I can go as far as I like; as far as is necessary to convince you we have to have Ralson – and fast!'

'Well, then tell me, and I too, will know secrets. I'll feel like a member of the Cabinet.'

'You'll know more than most. Look, Dr. Blaustein, let me explain it in lay language. So far, military advances have been made fairly equally in both offensive and defensive weapons. Once before there seemed to be a definite and permanent tipping of all warfare in the direction of the offense, and that was with the invention of gunpowder. But the defense caught up. The medieval man-in-armor-on-horse became the modern man-in-tank-on-treads, and the stone castle became the concrete pillbox. The same thing, you see, except that everything has been boosted several orders of magnitude.'

'Very good. You make it clear. But with the atomic bomb comes more orders of magnitude, no? You must go past concrete and steel for protection.'

'Right. Only we can't just make thicker and thicker walls. We've run out of materials that are strong enough. So we must abandon materials altogether. If the atom attacks, we must let the atom defend. We will use energy itself: a force field.'

'And what', asked Blaustein, gently, 'is a force field?'

'I wish I could tell you. Right now, it's an equation on paper. Energy can be so channeled as to create a wall of matterless inertia, theoretically. In practice, we don't know how to do it.'

'It would be a wall you could not go through, is that it? Even for atoms?'

'Even for atom bombs. The only limit on its strength would be the amount of energy we could pour into it. It could even theoretically be made to be impermeable to radiation. The gamma rays would bounce off it. What we're dreaming of is a screen that would be in permanent place about cities; at minimum strength, using practically no energy. It could then be triggered to maximum strength, using practically no energy. It could be triggered to maximum intensity in a fraction of a millisecond at the impingement of short-wave radiation; say the amount radiating from the mass of plutonium large enough to be an atomic war head. All this is theoretically possible.'

'And why must you have Ralson?'

'Because he is the only one who can reduce it to practice, if it can be made practical at all, quickly enough. Every minute counts these days. You know what the international situation is. Atomic defense *must* arrive before atomic war.'

'You are so sure of Ralson?'

'I am sure of him as I can be of anything. The man is amazing, Dr. Blaustein. He is always right. Nobody in the field knows how he does it.'

'A sort of intuition, no?' The psychiatrist looked disturbed. 'A kind of reasoning that goes beyond ordinary human capacities. Is that it?'

I make no pretense of knowing what it is.'

'Let me speak to him once more then. I will let you know.'

'Good.' Grant rose to leave; then, as if in afterthought, he said, 'I might say, Doctor, that if you don't do something, the Commission plans to take Dr. Ralson out of your hands.'

'And try another psychiatrist? If they wish to do that, of course, I will not stand in their way. It is my opinion, however, that no reputable practitioner will pretend there is a rapid cure.'

'We may not intend further mental treatment. He may simply be returned to work.'

'That, Dr. Grant, I will fight. You will get nothing out of him. It will be his death.'

'We get nothing out of him anyway.'

'This way there is at least a chance, no?'

'I hope so. And by the way, please don't mention the fact that I said anything about taking Ralson away.'

'I will not, and I thank you for the warning. Good-bye, Dr. Grant.'

'I made a fool of myself last time, didn't I, Doctor?' said Ralson. He was frowning.

'You mean you don't believe what you said then?'

'*I do!*' Ralson's slight form trembled with the intensity of his affirmation.

He rushed to the window, and Blaustein swiveled in his chair to keep him in view. There were bars in the window. He couldn't jump. The glass was unbreakable.

Twilight was ending, and the stars were beginning to come out. Ralson stared at them in fascination, then he turned to Blaustein and flung a finger outward. 'Every single one of them is an incubator. They maintain temperatures at the desired point. Different experiments; different temperatures. And the planets that circle them are just huge cultures, containing different nutrient mixtures and different life forms. The experimenters are economical, too — whatever and whoever they are. They've cultured many types of life forms in this particular test-tube. Dinosaurs in a moist, tropical age and ourselves among the glaciers. They turn the sun up and down and we try to work out the physics of it. Physics!' He drew his lips back in a snarl.

'Surely,' said Dr. Blaustein, 'it is not possible that the sun can be turned up and down at will.'

'Why not? It's just like a heating element in an oven. You think bacteria know what it is that works the heat that reaches them? Who knows? Maybe they evolve theories, too. Maybe they have their cosmogonies about cosmic catastrophes, in which clashing light-bulbs create strings of Petri dishes. Maybe they think there must be some beneficent creator that supplies them with food and warmth and says to them, "Be fruitful and multiply!"

'We breed like them, not knowing why. We obey the so-called laws of nature which are only our interpretation of the not-understood forces imposed upon us.

'And now they've got the biggest experiment of any yet on their hands. It's been going on for two hundred years. They decided to develop a strain for mechanical aptitude in England in the seventeen hundreds, I imagine. We call it the Industrial Revolution. It began with steam, went on to electricity, then atoms. It was an interesting experiment, but they took their chances on letting it spread. Which is why they'll have to be very drastic indeed in ending it.'

Blaustein said, 'And how would they plan to end it? Do you have an idea about that?'

'You ask *me* how they plan to end it. You can look about the world today and still ask what is likely to bring our technological age to an end. All the earth fears an atomic war and would do anything to avoid it; yet all the earth fears that an atomic war is inevitable.'

'In other words, the experimenters will arrange an atom war whether we want it or not, to kill off the technological era we are in, and to start afresh. That is it, no?'

'Yes. It's logical. When we sterilize an instrument, do the germs know where the killing heat comes from? Or what has brought it about? There is some way the experimenters can raise the heat of our emotions; some way they can handle us that passes our understanding.'

'Tell me,' said Blaustein, 'is that why you want to die? Because you think the destruction of civilization is coming and can't be stopped?'

Ralson said, 'I *don't* want to die. It's just that I must.' His eyes were tortured. 'Doctor, if you had a culture of germs that were highly dangerous and that you had to keep under absolute control, might you not have an agar medium impregnated with, say, penicillin, in a circle at a certain distance from the center of inoculation? Any germs spreading out too far from the center would die. You would have nothing against the particular germs who were killed; you might not even know that any germs had spread that far in the first place. It would be purely automatic.

'Doctor, there is a penicillin ring about our intellects. When we stray too far; when we penetrate the true meaning of our own existence, we have reached into the penicillin and we must die. It works slowly – but it's hard to stay alive.'

He smiled briefly and sadly. Then he said, 'May I go back to my room now, Doctor?'

Dr. Blaustein went to Ralson's room about noon the next day. It was a small room and featureless. The walls were gray with padding. Two small windows were high up and could not be reached. The mattress lay directly on the padded floor. There was nothing of metal in the room; nothing that could be utilized in tearing life from body. Even Ralson's nails were clipped short.

Ralson sat up. 'Hello!'

'Hello, Dr. Ralson. May I speak to you?'

'Here? There isn't any seat I can offer you.'

'It is all right. I'll stand. I have a sitting job and it is good for my sitting-down place that I should stand sometimes. Dr. Ralson, I have thought all night of what you told me yesterday and in the days before.'

'And now you are going to apply treatment to rid me of what you think are delusions.'

'No. It is just that I wish to ask questions and perhaps to point out some consequences of your theories which . . . you will forgive me? . . . you may not have thought of.'

'Oh?'

'You see, Dr. Ralson, since you have explained your theories, I, too, know what you know. Yet I have no feeling about suicide.'

'Belief is more than something intellectual, Doctor. You'd have to believe this with all your insides, which you don't.'

'Do you not think perhaps it is rather a phenomenon of adaptation?'

'How do you mean?'

'You are not really a biologist, Dr. Ralson. And although you are very brilliant indeed in physics, you do not think of everything with respect to these bacterial cultures you use as analogies. You know that it is possible to breed bacterial strains that are resistant to penicillin or to almost any bacterial poison.'

'Well?'

'The experimenters who breed us have been working with humanity for many generations, no? And this particular strain which they have been culturing for two centuries shows no sign of dying out spontaneously. Rather, it is a vigorous strain and a very infective one. Older high-culture strains were confined to single cities or to small areas and lasted only a generation or two. This one is spreading throughout the world. It is a *very* infective strain. Do you not think it may have developed penicillin immunity? In other words, the methods the experimenters use to wipe out the culture may not work too well any more, no?'

Ralson shook his head. 'It's working on me.'

'You are perhaps non-resistant. Or you have stumbled into a very high concentration of penicillin indeed. Consider all the people who have been trying to outlaw atomic warfare and to establish some form of world government and lasting peace. The effort has risen in recent years, without too awful results.'

'It isn't stopping the atomic war that's coming.'

'No, but maybe only a little more effort is all that is required. The peace-advocates do not kill themselves. More and more humans are immune to the experimenters. Do you know what they are doing in the laboratory?'

'I don't want to know.'

'You *must* know. They are trying to invent a force field that will stop the atom bomb. Dr. Ralson, if I am culturing a virulent and pathological bacterium; then, even with all precautions, it may sometimes happen that I will start a plague. We may be bacteria to them, but we are dangerous to them, also, or they wouldn't wipe us out so carefully after each experiment.

'They are not quick, no? To them a thousand years is a day, no? By the time they realize we are out of the culture, past the penicillin, it will be too late for them to stop us. They have brought us to the atom, and if we can only prevent ourselves from using it upon one another, we many turn out to be too much even for the experimenters.'

Ralson rose to his feet. Small though he was, he was an inch and a half taller than Blaustein. 'They are really working on a force field?'

'They are trying to. But they need you.'

'No. I can't.'

'They must have you in order that you might see what is so

obvious to you. It is not obvious to them. Remember, it is your help, or else – defeat of man by the experimenters.'

Ralson took a few rapid steps away, staring into the blank, padded wall. He muttered, 'But there must be that defeat. If they build a force field, it will mean death for all of them before it can be completed.'

'Some or all of them may be immune, no? And in any case, it will be death for them anyhow. They are trying.'

Ralson said, 'I'll try to help them.'

'Do you still want to kill yourself?'

'Yes.'

'But you'll try not to, no?'

'I'll *try* not to, Doctor.' His lip quivered. 'I'll have to be watched.'

Blaustein climbed the stairs and presented his pass to the guard in the lobby. He had already been inspected at the outer gate, but he, his pass, and its signature were now scrutinized once again. After a moment, the guard retired to his little booth and made a phone call. The answer satisfied him. Blaustein took a seat and, in half a minute, was up again, shaking hands with Dr. Grant.

'The President of the United States would have trouble getting in here, no?' said Blaustein.

The lanky physicist smiled. 'You're right, if he came without warning.'

They took an elevator which traveled twelve floors. The office to which Grant led the way had windows in three directions. It was sound-proofed and air-conditioned. Its walnut furniture was in a state of high polish.

Blaustein said, 'My goodness. It is like the office of the chairman of a board of directors. Science is becoming big business.'

Grant looked embarrassed. 'Yes, I know, but government money flows easily and it is difficult to persuade a congressman that your work is important unless he can see, smell, and touch the surface shine.'

Blaustein sat down and felt the upholstered seat give way slowly. He said, 'Dr. Elwood Ralson has agreed to return to work.'

'Wonderful. I was hoping you would say that. I was hoping that was why you wanted to see me.' As though inspired by the news, Grant offered the psychiatrist a cigar, which was refused.

'However,' said Blaustein, 'he remains a very sick man. He will have to be treated carefully and with insight.'

'Of course. Naturally.'

'It's not quite as simple as you may think. I want to tell you something of Ralson's problems, so that you will really understand how delicate the situation is.'

He went on talking and Grant listened first in concern, and then in astonishment. 'But then the man is out of his head, Dr. Blaustein. He'll be of no use to us. He's crazy.'

Blaustein shrugged. 'It depends on how you define "crazy". It's a bad word; don't use it. He has delusions, certainly. Whether they will affect his peculiar talents one cannot know.'

'But surely no sane man could possibly –'

'Please. Please. Let us not launch into long discussions on psychiatric definitions of sanity and so on. The man has delusions and, ordinarily, I would dismiss them from all consideration. It is just that I have been given to understand that the man's particular ability lies in his manner of proceeding to the solution of a problem by what seems to be outside ordinary reason. That is so, no?'

'Yes. That *must* be admitted.'

'How can you and I judge then as to the worth of one of his conclusions. Let me ask you, do *you* have suicidal impulses lately?'

'I don't think so.'

'And other scientists here?'

'No, of course not.'

'I would suggest, however, that while research on the force field proceeds, the scientists concerned be watched here and at home. It might even be a good enough idea that they should not go home. Offices like these could be arranged to be a small dormitory –'

'Sleep at work. You would never get them to agree.'

'Oh, yes. If you do not tell them the real reason but say it is for security purposes, they will agree. "Security purposes" is a wonderful phrase these days, no? Ralson must be watched more than anyone.'

'Of course.'

'But all this is minor. It is something to be done to satisfy my conscience in case Ralson's theories are correct. Actually, I don't believe them. They *are* delusions, but once that is granted, it is necessary to ask what the causes of those delusions are. What is it in Ralson's mind, in his background, in his life that makes it so necessary for him to have these particular delusions? One cannot answer that simply. It may well take years of constant psychoanalysis to discover the answer. And until the answer is discovered, he will not be cured.

'But, meanwhile, we can perhaps make intelligent guesses. He has had an unhappy childhood, which, in one way or another, has brought him face to face with death in very unpleasant fashion. In addition, he has never been able to form associations with other children, or, as he grew older, with other men. He was always impatient with their slower forms of reasoning. Whatever difference there is between his mind and that of others, it has built a wall between him and society as strong as the force field you are trying to design. For similar reasons, he has been unable to enjoy a normal sex life. He has never married; he has had no sweethearts.

'It is easy to see that he could easily compensate to himself for this failure to be accepted by his social milieu by taking refuge in the thought that other human beings are inferior to himself. Which is, of course, true, as far as mentality is concerned. There are, of course, many, many facets to the human personality and in not all of them is he superior. No one is. Others, then, who are more prone to see merely what is inferior, just as he himself is, would not accept his affected pre-eminence of position. They would think him queer, even laughable, which would make it even more important to Ralson to prove how miserable and inferior the human species was. How could he better do that than to show that mankind was simply a form of bacteria to other superior creatures which experiment upon them. And then his impulses to suicide would be a wild desire to break away completely from being a man at all; to stop this identification with the miserable species he has created in his mind. You see?'

Grant nodded. 'Poor guy.'

'Yes, it is a pity. Had he been properly taken care of in childhood – Well, it is best for Dr. Ralson that he have no contact with any of the other men here. He is too sick to be treated with them. You, yourself, must arrange to be the only man who will see him or speak to him. Dr. Ralson has agreed to that. He apparently thinks you are not as stupid as some of the others.'

Grant smiled faintly. 'That is agreeable to me.'

'You will, of course, be careful. I would not discuss anything with him but his work. If he should volunteer information about his theories, which I doubt, confine yourself to something non-committal, and leave. And at all times, keep away anything that is sharp and pointed. Do not let him reach a window. Try to have his hands kept in view. You understand. I leave my patient in your care, Dr. Grant.'

'I will do my best, Dr. Blaustein.'

For two months, Ralson lived in a corner of Grant's office, and Grant lived with him. Gridwork had been built up before the windows, wooden furniture was removed and upholstered sofas brought in. Ralson did his thinking on the couch and his calculating on a desk pad atop a hassock.

The 'Do Not Enter' was a permanent fixture outside the office. Meals were left outside. The adjoining men's room was marked off for private use and the door between it and the office removed. Grant switched to an electric razor. He made certain that Ralson took sleeping pills each night and waited till the other slept before sleeping himself.

And always reports were brought to Ralson. He read them while Grant watched and tried to seem not to watch.

Then Ralson would let them drop and stare at the ceiling, with one hand shading his eyes.

'Anything?' asked Grant.

Ralson shook his head from side to side.

Grant said, 'Look, I'll clear the building during the swing shift. It's important that you see some of the experimental jigs we've been setting up.'

They did so, wandering through the lighted, empty buildings like drifting ghosts, hand in hand. Always hand in hand. Grant's grip was tight. But after each trip, Ralson would still shake his head from side to side.

Half a dozen times he would begin writing; each time there would be a few scrawls and then he would kick the hassock over on its side.

Until, finally, he began writing once again and covered half a page rapidly. Automatically, Grant approached. Ralson looked up, covering the sheet of paper with a trembling hand.

He said, 'Call Blaustein.'

'What?'

'I said, "Call Blaustein." Get him here. Now!'

Grant moved to the telephone.

Ralson was writing rapidly now, stopping only to brush wildly at his forehead with the back of a hand. It came away wet.

He looked up and his voice was cracked. 'Is he coming?'

Grant looked worried. 'He isn't at his office.'

'Get him at his home. Get him wherever he is. *Use* that telephone. Don't play with it.'

Grant used it; and Ralson pulled another sheet toward himself.

Five minutes later, Grant said, 'He's coming. What's wrong? You're looking sick.'

Ralson could speak only thickly. 'No time – can't talk –'

He was writing, scribbling, scrawling, shakily diagraming. It was as though he were driving his hands, fighting it.

'Dictate!' urged Grant. 'I'll write.'

Ralson shook him off. His words were unintelligible. He held his wrist with his other hand, shoving it as though it were a piece of wood, and then he collapsed over the papers.

Grant edged them out from under him and laid Ralson down on the couch. He hovered over him restlessly and hopelessly until Blaustein arrived.

Blaustein took one look. 'What happened?'

Grant said, 'I think he's alive,' but by that time Blaustein had verified that for himself, and Grant told him what had happened.

Blaustein used a hypodermic and they waited. Ralson's eyes were blank when they opened. He moaned.

Blaustein leaned close. 'Ralson.'

Ralson's hands reached out blindly and clutched at the psychiatrist. 'Doc. Take me back.'

'I will. Now. It is that you have the force field worked out, no?'

'It's on the papers. Grant, it's on the papers.'

Grant had them and was leafing through them dubiously. Ralson said, weakly, 'It's not *all* there. It's all I can write. You'll *have* to make it out of that. Take me back, Doc!'

'Wait,' said Grant. He whispered urgently to Blaustein. 'Can't you leave him here till we test this thing? I can't make out what most of this is. The writing is illegible. Ask him what makes him think this will work.'

'Ask *him*?' said Blaustein, gently. 'Isn't he the one who always knows?'

'Ask me, anyway,' said Ralson, overhearing from where he lay on the couch. His eyes were suddenly wide and blazing.

They turned to him.

He said, '*They* don't want a force field. *They!* The experimenters! As long as I had no true grasp, things remained as they were. But I hadn't followed up that thought – *that* thought which is there in the papers – I hadn't followed it up for thirty seconds before I felt . . . I felt – Doctor –'

Blaustein said, 'What is it?'

Ralson was whispering again, 'I'm deeper in the penicillin. I could feel myself plunging in and in, the further I went with that. I've never been in . . . so deep. That's how I knew I was right. Take me away.'

Blaustein straightened. 'I'll have to take him away, Grant. There's no alternative. If you can make out what he's written, that's it. If you can't make it out, I can't help you. That man can do no more work in his field without dying, do you understand?'

'But', said Grant, 'he's dying of something imaginary.'

'All right. Say that he is. But he will be really dead just the same, no?'

Ralson was unconscious again and heard nothing of this. Grant looked at him somberly, then said, 'Well, take him away, then.'

Ten of the top men at the Institute watched glumly as slide after slide filled the illuminated screen. Grant faced them, expression hard and frowning.

He said, 'I think the idea is simple enough. You're mathematicians and you're engineers. The scrawl may seem illegible, but it was done with meaning behind it. That meaning must somehow remain in the writing, distorted though it is. The first page is clear enough. It should be a good lead. Each one of you will look at every page over and over again. You're going to put down every possible version of each page as it seems it might be. You will work independently. I want no consultations.'

One of them said, 'How do you know it means *anything*, Grant?'

'Because those are Ralson's notes.'

'*Ralson*? I thought he was –'

'You thought he was sick,' said Grant. He had to shout over

the rising hum of conversation. 'I know. He is. That's the writing of a man who was nearly dead. It's all we'll ever get from Ralson, any more. Somewhere in that scrawl is the answer to the force field problem. If we can't find it, we may have to spend ten years looking for it elsewhere.'

They bent to their work. The night passed. Two nights passed. Three nights –

Grant looked at the results. He shook his head. 'I'll take your word for it that it is all self-consistent. I can't say I understand it.'

Lowe, who, in the absence of Ralson, would readily have been rated the best nuclear engineer at the Institute, shrugged. 'It's not exactly clear to me. If it works, he hasn't explained why.'

'He had no time to explain. Can you build the generator as he describes it?'

'I could try.'

'Would you look at all the other versions of the pages?'

'The others are definitely not self-consistent.'

'Would you double-check?'

'Sure.'

'And could you start construction anyway?'

'I'll get the shop started. But I tell you frankly that I'm pessimistic.'

'I know. So am I.'

The thing grew. Hal Ross, Senior Mechanic, was put in charge of the actual construction, and he stopped sleeping. At any hour of the day or night, he could be found at it, scratching his bald head.

He asked questions only once, 'What is it, Dr. Lowe? Never saw anything like it. What's it supposed to do?'

Lowe said, 'You know where you are, Ross. You know we don't ask questions here. Don't ask again.'

Ross did not ask again. He was known to dislike the structure that was being built. He called it ugly and unnatural. But he stayed at it.

Blaustein called one day.

Grant said, 'How's Ralson?'

'Not good. He wants to attend the testing of the field projector he designed.'

Grant hesitated, 'I suppose he should. It's his after all.'
'I would have to come with him.'

Grant looked unhappier. 'It might be dangerous, you know. Even in a pilot test, we'd be playing with tremendous energies.'

Blaustein said, 'No more dangerous for us than for you.'

'Very well. The list of observers will have to be cleared through the Commission and the F.B.I., but I'll put you in.'

Blaustein looked about him. The field projector squatted in the very center of the huge testing laboratory, but all else had been cleared. There was no visible connection with the pluto-nium pile which served as energy-source, but from what the psy-chiatrist heard in scraps about him – he knew better than to ask Ralson – the connection was from beneath.

At first, the observers had circled the machine, talking in in-comprehensibles, but they were drifting away now. The gallery was filling up. There were at least three men in generals' uniform on the other side, and a real coterie of lower-scale military. Blau-stein chose an unoccupied portion of the railing: for Ralson's sake, most of all.

He said, 'Do you still think you would like to stay?'

It was warm enough within the laboratory, but Ralson was in his coat, with his collar turned up. It made little difference, Blau-stein felt. He doubted that any of Ralson's former acquaintances would now recognize him.

Ralson said, 'I'll stay.'

Blaustein was pleased. He wanted to see the test. He turned again at a new voice.

'Hello, Dr. Blaustein.'

For a minute, Blaustein did not place him, then he said, 'Ah, Inspector Darrity. What are you doing here?'

'Just what you would suppose.' He indicated the watchers. 'There isn't any way you can weed them out so that you can be sure there won't be any mistakes. I once stood as near to Klaus Fuchs as I am standing to you.' He tossed his pocketknife into the air and retrieved it with a dexterous motion.

'Ah, yes. Where shall one find perfect security? What man can trust even his own unconscious? And you will now stand near to me, no?'

'Might as well.' Darrity smiled. 'You were very anxious to get in here, weren't you?'

'Not for myself, Inspector. And would you put away the knife, please.'

Darrity turned in surprise in the direction of Blaustein's gentle head-gesture. He put his knife away and looked at Blaustein's companion for the second time. He whistled softly.

He said, 'Hello, Dr. Ralson.'

Ralson croaked, 'Hello.'

Blaustein was not surprised at Darrity's reaction. Ralson had lost twenty pounds since returning to the sanatorium. His face was yellow and wrinkled: the face of a man who had suddenly become sixty.

Blaustein said, 'Will the test be starting soon?'

Darrity said, 'It looks as if they're starting now.'

He turned and leaned on the rail. Blaustein took Ralson's elbow and began leading him away, but Darrity said, softly, 'Stay here, Doc. I don't want you wandering about.'

Blaustein looked across the laboratory. Men were standing about with the uncomfortable air of having turned half to stone. He could recognize Grant, tall and gaunt, moving his hand slowly to light a cigarette, then changing his mind and putting lighter and cigarette in his pocket. The young men at the control panels waited tensely.

Then there was a low humming and the faint smell of ozone filled the air.

Ralson said harshly, 'Look!'

Blaustein and Darrity looked along the pointing finger. The projector seemed to flicker. It was as though there were heated air rising between it and them. An iron ball came swinging down pendulum fashion and passed through the flickering area.

'It slowed up, no?' said Blaustein, excitedly.

Ralson nodded. 'They're measuring the height of rise on the other side to calculate the loss of momentum. Fools! I *said* it would work.' He was speaking with obvious difficulty.

Blaustein said, 'Just watch, Dr. Ralson. I would not allow myself to grow needlessly excited.'

The pendulum was stopped in its swinging, drawn up. The flickering about the projector became a little more intense and the iron sphere arced down once again.

Over and over again, and each time the sphere's motion was slowed with more of a jerk. It made a clearly audible sound as it struck the flicker. And eventually, it *bounced*. First, soggily, as though it hit putty, and then ringingly, as though it hit steel, so that the noise filled the place.

They drew back the pendulum bob and used it no longer. The projector could hardly be seen behind the haze that surrounded it.

Grant gave an order and the odor of ozone was suddenly sharp and pungent. There was a cry from the assembled observers; each one exclaiming to his neighbor. A dozen fingers were pointing.

Blaustein leaned over the railing, as excited as the rest. Where the projector had been, there was now only a huge semi-globular mirror. It was perfectly and beautifully clear. He could see himself in it, a small man standing on a small balcony that curved up on each side. He could see the fluorescent lights reflected in spots of glowing illumination. It was wonderfully sharp.

He was shouting, 'Look, Ralson. It is reflecting energy. It is reflecting light waves like a mirror. Ralson –'

He turned, 'Ralson! Inspector, where is Ralson?'

'What?' Darrity whirled. 'I haven't seen him.'

He looked about, wildly. 'Well, he won't get away. No way of getting out of here now. You take the other side.' And then he clapped hand to thigh, fumbled for a moment in his pocket, and said, 'My knife is gone.'

Blaustein found him. He was inside the small office belonging to Hal Ross. It led off the balcony, but under the circumstances, of course, it had been deserted. Ross himself was not even an observer. A senior mechanic need not observe. But his office would do very well for the final end of the long fight against suicide.

Blaustein stood in the doorway for a sick moment, then turned. He caught Darrity's eye as the latter emerged from a similar office a hundred feet down the balcony. He beckoned, and Darrity came at a run.

Dr. Grant was trembling with excitement. He had taken two puffs at each of two cigarettes and trodden each underfoot thereafter. He was fumbling with the third now.

He was saying, 'This is better than any of us could possibly have hoped. We'll have the gunfire test tomorrow. I'm sure of the result now, but we've planned it; we'll go through with it. We'll skip the small arms and start with the bazooka levels. Or maybe not. It might be necessary to construct a special testing structure to take care of the ricochet problem.'

He discarded his third cigarette.

A general said, 'We'd have to try a literal atom-bombing, of course.'

'Naturally. Arrangements have already been made to build a mock-city at Eniwetok. We could build a generator on the spot and drop the bomb. There'd be animals inside.'

'And you really think if we set up a field in full power it would hold the bomb?'

'It's not just that, General. There'd be no noticeable field at all until the bomb is dropped. The radiation of the plutonium would have to energize the field before explosion. As we did here in the last step. That's the essence of it all.'

'You know,' said a Princeton professor, 'I see disadvantages, too. When the field is on full, anything it protects is in total darkness, as far as the sun is concerned. Besides that, it strikes me that the enemy can adopt the practice of dropping harmless radioactive missiles to set off the field at frequent intervals. It would have nuisance value and be a considerable drain on our pile as well.'

'Nuisances', said Grant, 'can be survived. These difficulties will be met eventually, I'm sure, now that the main problem has been solved.'

The British observer had worked his way toward Grant and was shaking hands. He said, 'I feel better about London already. I cannot help but wish your government would allow me to see the complete plans. What I have seen strikes me as completely ingenious. It seems obvious now, of course, but how did anyone ever come to think of it?'

Grant smiled. 'That question has been asked before with reference to Dr. Ralson's devices –'

He turned at the touch of a hand upon his shoulder. 'Dr. Blaustein! I had nearly forgotten. Here, I want to talk to you.'

He dragged the small psychiatrist to one side and hissed in his ear, 'Listen, can you persuade Ralson to be introduced to these people? This is his triumph.'

Blaustein said, 'Ralson is dead.'

'*What!*'

'Can you leave these people for a time?'

'Yes ... yes – Gentlemen, you will excuse me for a few minutes?'

He hurried off with Blaustein.

The Federal men had already taken over. Unobtrusively, they barred the doorway to Ross's office. Outside there were the milling crowd discussing the answer to Alamogordo that they had just witnessed. Inside, unknown to them, was the death of the answerer. The G-man barrier divided to allow Grant and Blaustein to enter. It closed behind them again.

For a moment, Grant raised the sheet. He said, 'He looks peaceful.'

'I would say – happy,' said Blaustein.

Darrity said, colorlessly, 'The suicide weapon was my own knife. It was my negligence; it will be reported as such.'

'No, no,' said Blaustein, 'that would be useless. He was my patient and I am responsible. In any case, he would not have lived another week. Since he invented the projector, he was a dying man.'

Grant said, 'How much of this has to be placed in the Federal files? Can't we forget all about his madness?'

'I'm afraid not, Dr. Grant,' said Darrity.

'I have told him the whole story,' said Blaustein, sadly.

Grant looked from one to the other. 'I'll speak to the Director. I'll go to the President, if necessary. I don't see that there need be any mention of suicide or of madness. He'll get full publicity as inventor of the field projector. It's the least we can do for him.' His teeth were gritting.

Blaustein said, 'He left a note.'

'A note?'

Darrity handed him a sheet of paper and said, 'Suicides almost always do. This is one reason the doctor told me about what really killed Ralson.'

The note was addressed to Blaustein and it went:

'The projector works; I knew it would. The bargain is done. You've got it and you don't need me any more. So I'll go. You needn't worry about the human race, Doc. You were right. They've bred us too long; they've taken too many chances. We're out of the culture now and they won't be able to stop us. I know. That's all I can say. I know.'

He had signed his name quickly and then underneath there was one scrawled line, and it said:

'Provided enough men are penicillin-resistant.'

Grant made a motion to crumple the paper, but Darrity held out a quick hand.

'For the record, Doctor,' he said.

Grant gave it to him and said, 'Poor Ralson! He died believing all that trash.'

Blaustein nodded. 'So he did. Ralson will be given a great funeral, I suppose, and the fact of his invention will be publicized without the madness and the suicide. But the government men will remain interested in his mad theories. They may not be so mad, no, Mr. Darrity?'

'That's ridiculous, Doctor,' said Grant. 'There isn't a scientist on the job who has shown the least uneasiness about it at all.'

'Tell him, Mr. Darrity,' said Blaustein.

Darrity said, 'There has been another suicide. No, no, none of the scientists. No one with a degree. It happened this morning, and we investigated because we thought it might have some connection with today's test. There didn't seem any, and we were going to keep it quiet till the test was over. Only now there seems to be a connection.

'The man who died was just a guy with a wife and three kids. No reason to die. No history of mental illness. He threw himself under a car. We have witnesses, and it's certain he did it on purpose. He didn't die right away and they got a doctor to him. He was horribly mangled, but his last words were "I feel much better now" and he died.'

'But who was he?' cried Grant.

'Hal Ross. The guy who actually built the projector. The guy whose office this is.'

Blaustein walked to the window. The evening sky was darkening into starriness.

He said, 'The man knew nothing about Ralson's views. He had never spoken to Ralson, Mr. Darrity tells me. Scientists are probably resistant as a whole. They must be or they are quickly driven out of the profession. Ralson was an exception, a penicillin-sensitive who insisted on remaining. You see what happened to him. But what about the others: those who have remained in walks of life where there is no constant weeding out of the sensitive ones. How much of humanity *is* penicillin-resistant?'

'You *believe* Ralson?' asked Grant in horror.
'I don't really know.'
Blaustein looked at the stars.
Incubators?

In 1951, the Korean War broke out and that was a depressing time indeed, almost as depressing as the present. I will not conceal from you that I am not enthusiastic over what Othello called 'quality, pride, pomp, and circumstance of glorious war'.

World War II had been something unique. That was one war there could be few idealistic qualms over. We were fighting an absolute evil that seemed quite beyond the usual defame-the-enemy routine; and there seemed a reasonable hope that once the war was over there would be some way of setting up a form of world organization to prevent future wars.

The euphoria of the days of the immediate end of the war and of the setting up of the United Nations didn't last long and the Korean War spelled final ruin to the first great hopes.

You might think that we science fiction writers were luckier than most. We had so nice a way of 'escaping'. Off we could go into space, leaving the Earth-bound problems of the day behind us. Well, escape isn't that easy. It is harder than you think to divorce yourself from reality, and when, in the days of Korea, I blasted off in my spaceship for the empty distances between the stars, what did I find? An interstellar war, a battle for a spaceship.

I wasn't escaping at all!

But one more thing. Before the days of television there was something called radio, and in the late 1940s and early 1950s, we had science fiction on it. Radio didn't have the problem of the complicated and expensive sets that television requires in order to give a semblance of reality to science fiction. It can do everything with sound effects, and the proper sounds can be made into the most bizarre visual effects in the mind.

The programs involved – 'Two Thousand Plus' and 'Dimension X' – were, unfortunately, not heavily sponsored when they were sponsored at all and they did not last long, but while they were on, they were intensely satisfying to me. What's more, they ran no less than three of my stories. One of them was 'Nightfall' (of course), and a second was 'C-Chute.'

In the radio version of 'C-Chute,' Mullen was played by an actor with a distinctive voice – dry, restrained, unemotional, and gentle. It was exactly Mullen's voice. Once television came in, I found that voice, and matched the face to it, and that looked like Mullen.

It is so pleasant, every time I see him, to be able to say (despite

the fact that he is a fairly tall man), 'There's Mullen.' Mullen is
the only one of all my characters I have seen in the flesh, and I
have carefully refrained from ever finding out the actor's real
name. I want him to remain Mullen.

First appearance – Galaxy Science Fiction, *October 1951, by*
Galaxy Publishing Corporation.

C-CHUTE

Even from the cabin into which he and the other passengers had
been herded, Colonel Anthony Windham could still catch the
essence of the battle's progress. For a while, there was silence, no
jolting, which meant the space-ships were fighting at astronomic-
al distance in a duel of energy blasts and powerful force-field
defenses.

He knew that could have only one end. Their Earth ship was
only an armed merchantman and his glimpse of the Kloro enemy
just before he had been cleared off deck by the crew was sufficient
to show it to be a light cruiser.

And in less than half an hour, there came those hard little
shocks he was waiting for. The passengers swayed back and forth
as the ship pitched and veered, as though it were an ocean liner
in a storm. But space was calm and silent as ever. It was their
pilot sending desperate bursts of steam through the steam-tubes,
so that by reaction the ship would be sent rolling and tumbling.
It could only mean that the inevitable had occurred. The Earth
ship's screens had been drained and it no longer dared withstand
a direct hit.

Colonel Windham tried to steady himself with his aluminium
cane. He was thinking that he was an old man; that he had spent
his life in the militia and had never seen a battle; that now, with
a battle going on around him, he was old and fat and lame and
had no men under his command.

They would be boarding soon, those Kloro monsters. It was

their way of fighting. They would be handicapped by spacesuits and their casualties would be high, but they wanted the Earth ship. Windham considered the passengers. For a moment, he thought, *if they were armed and I could lead them* –

He abandoned the thought. Porter was in an obvious state of funk and the young boy, Leblanc, was hardly better. The Polyorketes brothers – dash it, he *couldn't* tell them apart – huddled in a corner speaking only to one another. Mullen was a different matter. He sat perfectly erect, with no signs of fear or any other emotion in his face. But the man was just about five feet tall and had undoubtedly never held a gun of any sort in his hands in all his life. He could do nothing.

And there was Stuart, with his half-frozen smile and the high-pitched sarcasm which saturated all he said. Windham looked sidelong at Stuart now as Stuart sat there, pushing his dead-white hands through his sandy hair. With those artificial hands he was useless, anyway.

Windham felt the shuddering vibration of ship-to-ship contact; and in five minutes, there was the noise of the fight through the corridors. One of the Polyorketes brothers screamed and dashed for the door. The other called, 'Aristides! Wait!' and hurried after.

It happened so quickly. Aristides was out the door and into the corridors. One of the Polyorketes brothers screamed and briefly and there was never even a scream. Windham, from the doorway, turned in horror at the blackened stump of what was left. Strange – a lifetime in uniform and he had never before seen a man killed in violence.

It took the combined force of the rest to carry the other brother back struggling into the room.

The noise of battle subsided.

Stuart said, 'That's it. They'll put a prize crew of two aboard and take us to one of their home planets. We're prisoners of war, naturally.'

'Only two of the Kloros will stay aboard?' asked Windham, astonished.

Stuart said, 'It is their custom. Why do you ask, Colonel? Thinking of leading a gallant raid to retake the ship?'

Windham flushed. 'Simply a point of information, dash it.' But the dignity and tone of authority he tried to assume failed him, he knew. He was simply an old man with a limp.

And Stuart was probably right. He had lived among the Kloros and knew their ways.

John Stuart had claimed from the beginning that the Kloros were gentlemen. Twenty-four hours of imprisonment had passed, and now he repeated the statement as he flexed the fingers of his hands and watched the crinkles come and go in the soft artiplasm.

He enjoyed the unpleasant reaction it aroused in the others. People were made to be punctured; windy bladders, all of them. And they had hands of the same stuff as their bodies.

There was Anthony Windham, in particular. Colonel Windham, he called himself, and Stuart was willing to believe it. A retired colonel who had probably drilled a home guard militia on a village green, forty years ago, with such lack of distinction that he was not called back to service in any capacity, even during the emergency of Earth's first interstellar war.

'Dashed unpleasant thing to be saying about the enemy, Stuart. Don't know that I like your attitude.' Windham seemed to push the words through his clipped mustache. His head had been shaven, too, in imitation of the current military style, but now a gray stubble was beginning to show about a centered bald patch. His flabby cheeks dragged downward. That and the fine red lines on his thick nose gave him a somewhat undone appearance, as though he had been wakened too suddenly and too early in the morning.

Stuart said, 'Nonsense. Just reverse the present situation. Suppose an Earth warship had taken a Kloro liner. What do you think would have happened to any Kloro civilians aboard?'

'I'm sure the Earth fleet would observe all the interstellar rules of war,' Windham said stiffly.

'Except that there aren't any. If we landed a prize crew on one of their ships, do you think we'd take the trouble to maintain a chlorine atmosphere for the benefit of the survivors; allow them to keep their non-contraband possessions; give them the use of the most comfortable stateroom, etcetera, etcetera, etcetera?'

Ben Porter said, 'Oh, shut up, for God's sake. If I hear your etcetera, etcetera once again, I'll go nuts.'

Stuart said, 'Sorry!' He wasn't.

Porter was scarcely responsible. His thin face and beaky nose glistened with perspiration, and he kept biting the inside of his cheek until he suddenly winced. He put his tongue against the sore spot, which made him look even more clownish.

Stuart was growing weary of baiting them. Windham was too flabby a target and Porter could do nothing but writhe. The rest were silent. Demetrios Polyorketes was off in a world of silent internal grief for the moment. He had not slept the night before, most probably. At least, whenever Stuart woke to change his position – he himself had been rather restless – there had been Polyorketes' thick mumble from the next cot. It said many things, but the moan to which it returned over and over again was, 'Oh, my brother!'

He sat dumbly on his cot now, his red eyes rolling at the other prisoners out of his broad swarthy, unshaven face. As Stuart watched, his face sank into calloused palms so that only his mop of crisp and curly hair could be seen. He rocked gently, but now that they were all awake, he made no sound.

Claude Leblanc was trying very unsuccessfully to read a letter. He was the youngest of the six, scarcely out of college, returning to Earth to get married. Stuart had found him that morning weeping quietly, his pink and white face flushed and blotched as though it were a heartbroken child's. He was very fair, with almost a girl's beauty about his large blue eyes and full lips. Stuart wondered what kind of girl it was who had promised to be his wife. He had seen her picture. Who on the ship had not? She had the characterless prettiness that makes all pictures of fiancées indistinguishable. It seemed to Stuart that if he were a girl, however, he would want someone a little more pronouncedly masculine.

That left only Randolph Mullen. Stuart frankly did not have the least idea what to make of him. He was the only one of the six that had been on the Arcturian worlds for any length of time. Stuart, himself, for instance, had been there only long enough to give a series of lectures on astronautical engineering at the provincial engineering institute. Colonel Windham had been on a Cook's tour; Porter was trying to buy concentrated alien vegetables for his canneries on Earth; and the Polyorketes brothers had attempted to establish themselves in Arcturus as truck farmers and, after two growing seasons, gave it up, had somehow unloaded at a profit, and were returning to Earth.

Randolph Mullen, however, had been in the Arcturian system for seventeen years. How did voyagers discover so much about one another so quickly? As far as Stuart knew, the little man had scarcely spoken aboard ship. He was unfailingly polite, always stepped to one side to allow another to pass, but his entire vocabulary appeared to consist only of 'Thank you' and 'Pardon me.' Yet the word had gone around that this was his first trip to Earth in seventeen years.

He was a little man, very precise, almost irritatingly so. Upon awaking that morning, he had made his cot neatly, shaved, bathed and dressed. The habit of years seemed not in the least disturbed by the fact that he was a prisoner of the Kloros now. He was unobtrusive about it, it had to be admitted, and gave no impression of disapproving of the sloppiness of the others. He simply sat there, almost apologetic, trussed in his overconservative clothing, and hands loosely clasped in his lap. The thin line of hair on his upper lip, far from adding character to his face, absurdly increased its primness.

He looked like someone's idea of a caricature of a bookkeeper. And the queer thing about it all, Stuart thought, was that that was exactly what he was. He had noticed it on the registry — Randolph Fluellen Mullen; occupation, bookkeeper; employers, Prime Paper Box Co.; 27 Tobias Avenue, New Warsaw, Arcturus II.

'Mr. Stuart?'

Stuart looked up. It was Leblanc, his lower lip trembling slightly. Stuart tried to remember how one went about being gentle. He said, 'What is it, Leblanc?'

'Tell me, when will they let us go?'

'How should I know?'

'Everyone says you lived on a Kloro planet, and just now you said they were gentlemen.'

'Well, yes. But even gentlemen fight wars in order to win. Probably, we'll be interned for the duration.'

'But that could be *years*! Margaret is waiting. She'll think I'm *dead*!'

'I suppose they'll allow messages to be sent through once we're on their planet.'

Porter's hoarse voice sounded in agitation. 'Look here, if you know so much about these devils, what will they do to us while we're interned? What will they feed us? Where will they get oxygen for us? They'll kill us, I tell you.' And as an afterthought, 'I've got a wife waiting for me, too,' he added.

But Stuart had heard him speaking of his wife in the days before the attack. He wasn't impressed. Porter's nail-bitten fingers were pulling and plucking at Stuart's sleeve. Stuart drew away in sharp revulsion. He couldn't stand those ugly hands. It angered him to desperation that such monstrosities should be real while his own white and perfectly shaped hands were only mocking imitations grown out of an alien latex.

He said, 'They won't kill us. If they were going to, they would have done it before now. Look, we capture Kloros too, you know, and it's just a matter of common sense to treat your prisoners decently if you want the other side to be decent to your men. They'll do their best. The food may not be very good, but they're better chemists than we are. It's what they're best at. They'll know exactly what food factors we'll need and how many calories. We'll live. They'll see to that.'

Windham rumbled, 'You sound more and more like a blasted greenie sympathizer, Stuart. It turns my stomach to hear an Earthman speak well of the green fellas the way you've been doing. Burn it, man, where's your loyalty?'

'My loyalty's where it belongs. With honesty and decency, regardless of the shape of the being it appears in.' Stuart held up his hands. 'See these? Kloros made them. I lived on one of their planets for six months. My hands were mangled in the conditioning machinery of my own quarters. I thought the oxygen supply they gave me was a little poor – it wasn't, by the way – and I tried making the adjustments on my own. It was my fault. You should never trust yourself with the machines of another culture. By the time someone among the Kloros could put on an atmosphere suit and get to me, it was too late to save my hands.

'They grew these artiplasm things for me and operated. You know what that meant? It meant designing equipment and nutrient solutions that would work in oxygen atmosphere. It meant that their surgeons had to perform a delicate operation while dressed in atmosphere suits. And now I've got hands again.' He laughed harshly, and clenched them into weak fists. 'Hands –'

Windham said, 'And you'd sell your loyalty to Earth for that?'

'Sell my loyalty? You're mad. For years, I hated the Kloros for this. I was a master pilot on the Trans-Galactic Spacelines before it happened. Now? Desk job. Or an occasional lecture. It took me a long time to pin the fault on myself and to realize that the only role played by the Kloros was a decent one. They have their code of ethics, and it's as good as ours. If it weren't for the stupidity of some of their people – and, by God, of some of ours – we wouldn't be at war. And after it's over –'

Polyorketes was on his feet. His thick fingers curved inward before him and his dark eyes glittered. 'I don't like what you say, mister.'

'Why don't you?'

'Because you talk too nice about these damned green bastards. The Kloros were good to you, eh? Well, they weren't good to my brother. They killed him. I think maybe I kill you, you damned greenie spy.'

And he charged.

Stuart barely had time to raise his arms to meet the infuriated farmer. He gasped out, 'What the hell –' as he caught one wrist and heaved a shoulder to block the other which groped toward his throat.

His artiplasm hand gave way. Polyorketes wrenched free with scarcely an effort.

Windham was bellowing incoherently, and Leblanc was calling out in his reedy voice, 'Stop it! Stop it!' But it was little Mullen who threw his arms about the farmer's neck from behind and pulled with all his might. He was not very effective; Polyorketes seemed scarcely aware of the little man's weight upon his back. Mullen's feet left the floor so that he tossed helplessly to right and left. But he held his grip and it hampered Polyorketes sufficiently to allow Stuart to break free long enough to grasp Windham's aluminium cane.

He said, 'Stay away, Polyorketes.'

He was gasping for breath and fearful of another rush. The hollow aluminium cylinder was scarcely heavy enough to accomplish much, but it was better than having only his weak hands to defend himself with.

Mullen had loosed his hold and was now circling cautiously, his breathing roughened and his jacket in disarray.

Polyorketes, for a moment, did not move. He stood there, his shaggy head bent low. Then he said, 'It is no use. I must kill Kloros. Just watch your tongue, Stuart. If it keeps on rattling too much, you're liable to get hurt. Really hurt, I mean.'

Stuart passed a forearm over his forehead and thrust the cane back at Windham, who seized it with his left hand, while mopping his bald pate vigorously with a handkerchief in his right.

Windham said, 'Gentlemen, we must avoid this. It lowers our prestige. We must remember the common enemy. We are Earthmen and we must act what we are – the ruling race of the Galaxy. We dare not demean ourselves before the lesser breeds.'

'Yes, Colonel,' said Stuart, wearily. 'Give us the rest of the speech tomorrow.'

He turned to Mullen, 'I want to say thanks.'

He was uncomfortable about it, but he had to. The little accountant had surprised him completely.

But Mullen said, in a dry voice that scarcely raised above a whisper, 'Don't thank me, Mr. Stuart. It was the logical thing to do. If we are to be interned, we would need you as an interpreter, perhaps, one who would understand the Kloros.'

Stuart stiffened. It was, he thought, too much of the bookkeeper type of reasoning, too logical, too dry of juice. Present risk and ultimate advantage. The assets and debits balanced neatly. He would have liked Mullen to leap to his defense out of – well, out of what? Out of pure, unselfish decency?

Stuart laughed silently at himself. He was beginning to expect idealism of human beings, rather than good, straightforward, self-centered motivation.

Polyorketes was numb. His sorrow and rage were like acid inside him, but they had no words to get out. If he were Stuart, big-mouth, white-hands Stuart, he could talk and talk and maybe feel better. Instead, he had to sit there with half of him dead; with no brother, no Aristides –

It had happened so quickly. If he could only go back and have one second more warning, so that he might snatch Aristides, hold him, save him.

But mostly he hated the Kloros. Two months ago, he had hardly ever heard of them, and now he hated them so hard, he would be glad to die if he could kill a few.

He said, without looking up, 'What happened to start this war, eh?'

He was afraid Stuart's voice would answer. He hated Stuart's voice. But it was Windham, the bald one.

Windham said, 'The immediate cause, sir, was a dispute over

mining concessions in the Wyandotte system. The Kloros had poached on Earth property.'

'Room for both, Colonel!'

Polyorketes looked up at that, snarling. Stuart could not be kept quiet for long. He was speaking again; the cripple-hand, wiseguy, Kloros-lover.

Stuart was saying, 'Is that anything to fight over, Colonel? We can't use one another's worlds. Their chlorine planets are useless to us and our oxygen ones are useless to them. Chlorine is deadly to us and oxygen is deadly to them. There's no way we could maintain permanent hostility. Our races just don't coincide. Is there reason to fight then because both races want to dig iron out of the same airless planetoids when there are millions like them in the Galaxy?'

Windham said, 'There is the question of planetary honor –'

'Planetary fertilizer. How can it excuse a ridiculous war like this one? It can only be fought on outposts. It has to come down to a series of holding actions and eventually be settled by negotiations that might just as easily have been worked out in the first place. Neither we nor the Kloros will gain a thing.'

Grudgingly, Polyorketes found that he agreed with Stuart. What did he and Aristides care where Earth or the Kloros got their iron?

Was that something for Aristides to die over?

The little warning buzzer sounded.

Polyorketes' head shot up and he rose slowly, his lips drawing back. Only one thing could be at the door. He waited, arms tense, fists balled. Stuart was edging toward him. Polyorketes saw that and laughed to himself. Let the Kloro come in, and Stuart, along with all the rest, could not stop him.

Wait, Aristides, wait just a moment, and a fraction of revenge will be paid back.

The door opened and a figure entered, completely swathed in a shapeless, billowing travesty of a spacesuit.

An odd, unnatural, but not entirely unpleasant voice began, 'It is with some misgivings, Earthmen, that my companion and myself –'

It ended abruptly as Polyorketes, with a roar, charged once again. There was no science in the lunge. It was sheer bull-momentum. Dark head low, burly arms spread out with the hair-tufted fingers in choking position, he clumped on. Stuart was whirled to one side before he had a chance to intervene, and was spun tumbling across a cot.

The Kloro might have, without undue exertion, straight-armed Polyorketes to a halt, or stepped aside, allowing the whirlwind to pass. He did neither. With a rapid movement, a hand-weapon was up and a gentle pinkish line of radiance connected it with the plunging Earthman. Polyorketes stumbled and crashed down, his body maintaining its last curved position, one foot raised, as though a lightning paralysis had taken place. It toppled to one side and he lay there, eyes all alive and wild with rage.

The Kloro said, 'He is not permanently hurt.' He seemed not to resent the offered violence. Then he began again, 'It is with some misgiving, Earthmen, that my companion and myself were made aware of a certain commotion in this room. Are you in any need which we can satisfy?'

Stuart was angrily nursing his knee which he had scraped in colliding with the cot. He said, 'No, thank you, Kloro.'

'Now, look here,' puffed Windham, 'this is a dashed outrage. We demand that our release be arranged.'

The Kloro's tiny, insectlike head turned in the fat old man's direction. He was not a pleasant sight to anyone unused to him. He was about the height of an Earthman, but the top of him consisted of a thin stalk of a neck with a head that was the merest swelling. It consisted of a blunt triangular proboscis in front and two bulging eyes on either side. That was all. There was no brain pan and no brain. What corresponded to the brain in a Kloro was located in what would be an Earthly abdomen, leaving the head as a mere sensory organ. The Kloro's spacesuit followed the outlines of the head more or less faithfully, the two eyes being exposed by two clear semicircles of glass, which looked faintly green because of the chlorine atmosphere inside.

One of the eyes was now cocked squarely at Windham, who quivered uncomfortably under the glance, but insisted, 'You have no right to hold us prisoner. We are noncombatants.'

The Kloro's voice, sounding thoroughly artificial, came from a small attachment of chromium mesh on what served as its chest. The voice box was manipulated by compressed air under the control of one or two of the many delicate, forked tendrils that radiated from two circles about its upper body and were, mercifully enough, hidden by the suit.

The voice said, 'Are you serious, Earthman? Surely you have heard of war and rules of war and prisoners of war.'

It looked about, shifting eyes with quick jerks of its head, staring at a particular object first with one, then with another. It was Stuart's understanding that each eye transferred a separate message to the abdominal brain, which had to coordinate the two to obtain full information.

Windham had nothing to say. No one had. The Kloro, its four main limbs, roughly arms and legs in pairs, had a vaguely human appearance under the masking of the suit, if you looked no higher than its chest, but there was no way of telling what it felt.

They watched it turn and leave.

Porter coughed and said in a strangled voice, 'God, smell that chlorine. If they don't do something, we'll all die of rotted lungs.'

Stuart said, 'Shut up. There isn't enough chlorine in the air to make a mosquito sneeze, and what there is will be swept out in two minutes. Besides, a little chlorine is good for you. It may kill your cold virus.'

Windham coughed and said, 'Stuart, I feel that you might have said something to your Kloro friend about releasing us. You are scarcely as bold in their presence, dash it, as you are once they are gone.'

'You heard what the creature said, Colonel. We're prisoners of war, and prisoner exchanges are negotiated by diplomats. We'll just have to wait.'

Leblanc, who had turned pasty white at the entrance of the Kloro, rose and hurried into the privy. There was the sound of retching.

An uncomfortable silence fell while Stuart tried to think of something to say to cover the unpleasant sound. Mullen filled in. He had rummaged through a little box he had taken from under his pillow.

He said, 'Perhaps Mr. Leblanc had better take a sedative before retiring. I have a few. I'd be glad to give him one.' He explained his generosity immediately, 'Otherwise he may keep the rest of us awake, you see.'

'Very logical,' said Stuart, dryly. 'You'd better save one for Sir Launcelot here; save half a dozen.' He walked to where Polyorketes still sprawled and knelt at his side. 'Comfortable, baby?'

Windham said, 'Deuced poor taste speaking like that, Stuart.'

'Well, if you're so concerned about him, why don't you and Porter hoist him onto his cot?'

He helped them do so. Polyorketes' arms were trembling erratically now. From what Stuart knew of the Kloro's nerve weapons, the man should be in an agony of pins and needles about now.

Stuart said, 'And don't be too gentle with him, either. The damned fool might have gotten us all killed. And for what?'

He pushed Polyorketes' stiff carcass to one side and sat at the edge of the cot. He said, 'Can you hear me, Polyorketes?'

Polyorketes' eyes gleamed. An arm lifted abortively and fell back.

'Okay then, listen. Don't try anything like that again. The next time it may be the finish for all of us. If you had been a Kloro and he had been an Earthman, we'd be dead now. So just get one thing through your skull. We're sorry about your brother and it's a rotten shame, but it was his own fault.'

Polyorketes tried to heave and Stuart pushed him back.

'No, you keep on listening,' he said. 'Maybe this is the only time I'll get to talk to you when you *have* to listen. Your brother had no right leaving passengers' quarters. There was no place for him to go. He just got in the way of our own men. We don't even know for certain that it was a Kloro gun that killed him. It might have been one of our own.'

'Oh, I say, Stuart,' objected Windham.

Stuart whirled at him. 'Do you have proof it wasn't? Did you see the shot? Could you tell from what was left of the body whether it was Kloro energy or Earth energy?'

Polyorketes found his voice, driving his unwilling tongue into a fuzzy verbal snarl. 'Damned stinking greenie bastard.'

'Me?' said Stuart. 'I know what's going on in your mind, Polyorketes. You think that when the paralysis wears off, you'll ease your feelings by slamming me around. Well, if you do, it will probably be curtains for all of us.'

He rose, put his back against the wall. For the moment, he was fighting all of them. 'None of you know the Kloros the way I do. The physical differences you see are not important. The differences in their temperament are. They don't understand our views on sex, for instance. To them, it's just a biological reflex like breathing. They attach no importance to it. But they *do* attach importance to social groupings. Remember, their evolutionary ancestors had lots in common with our insects. They always assume that any group of Earthmen they find together makes up a social unit.

'That means just about everything to them. I don't understand exactly *what* it means. No Earthman can. But the result is that they never break up a group, just as we don't separate a mother and her children if we can help it. One of the reasons they may be treating us with kid gloves right now is that they imagine we're all broken up over the fact that they killed one of us, and they feel guilt about it.

'But this is what you'll have to remember. We're going to be interned together and *kept* together for duration. I don't like the thought. I wouldn't have picked any of you for co-internees and I'm pretty sure none of you would have picked me. But there it is. The Kloros could never understand that our being together on the ship is only accidental.

'That means we've got to get along somehow. That's not just goodie-goodie talk about birds in their little nest agreeing. What do you think would have happened if the Kloros had come in earlier and found Polyorketes and myself trying to kill each other? You don't know? Well, what do you suppose *you* would think of a mother you caught trying to kill her children?

'That's it, then. They would have killed every one of us as a bunch of Kloro-type perverts and monsters. Got that? How about you, Polyorketes? Have *you* got it? So let's call names if we have to, but let's keep our hands to ourselves. And now, if none of you mind, I'll massage my hands back into shape – these synthetic hands that I got from the Kloros and that one of my own kind tried to mangle again.'

For Claude Leblanc, the worst was over. He had been sick enough; sick with many things; but sick most of all over having ever left Earth. It had been a great thing to go to college off Earth. It had been an adventure and had taken him away from his mother. Somehow, he had been sneakingly glad to make that escape after the first month of frightened adjustment.

And then on the summer holidays, he had been no longer Claude, the shy-spoken scholar, but Leblanc, space traveler. He had swaggered the fact for all it was worth. It made him feel such a man to talk of stars and Jumps and the customs and environments of other worlds; it had given him courage with Margaret. She had loved him for the dangers he had undergone –

Except that this had been the first one, really, and he had not done so well. He knew it and was ashamed and wished he were like Stuart.

He used the excuse of mealtime to approach. He said, 'Mr. Stuart.'

Stuart looked up and said shortly, 'How do you feel?'

Leblanc felt himself blush. He blushed easily and the effort not to blush only made it worse. He said, 'Much better, thank you. We are eating. I thought I'd bring you your ration.'

Stuart took the offered can. It was standard space ration; thoroughly synthetic, concentrated, nourishing and, somehow, unsatisfying. It heated automatically when the can was opened, but could be eaten cold, if necessary. Though a combined fork-spoon utensil was enclosed, the ration was of a consistency that made the use of fingers practical and not particularly messy.

Stuart said, 'Did you hear my little speech?'

'Yes, sir. I want you to know you can count on me.'

'Well, good. Now go and eat.'

'May I eat here?'

'Suit yourself.'

For a moment, they ate in silence, and then Leblanc burst out, 'You are so sure of yourself, Mr. Stuart! It must be very wonderful to be like that!'

'Sure of myself? Thanks, but there's your self-assured one.'

Leblanc followed the direction of the nod in surprise. 'Mr. Mullen? That little man? Oh, no!'

'You don't think he's self-assured?'

Leblanc shook his head. He looked at Stuart intently to see if he could detect humor in his expression. 'That one is just cold. He has no emotion in him. He's like a little machine. I find him repulsive. You're different, Mr. Stuart. You have it all inside, but you control it. I would like to be like that.'

And as though attracted by the magnetism of the mention, even though unheard, of his name, Mullen joined them. His can of ration was barely touched. It was still steaming gently as he squatted opposite them.

His voice had its usual quality of furtively rustling underbrush. 'How long, Mr. Stuart, do you think the trip will take?'

'Can't say, Mullen. They'll undoubtedly be avoiding the usual trade routes and they'll be making more Jumps through hyperspace than usual to throw off possible pursuit. I wouldn't be surprised if it took as long as a week. Why do you ask? I presume you have a very practical and logical reason?'

'Why, yes. Certainly.' He seemed quite shellbacked to sarcasm. He said, 'It occurred to me that it might be wise to ration the rations, so to speak.'

'We've got enough food and water for a month. I checked on that first thing.'

'I see. In that case, I will finish the can.' He did, using the all-purpose utensil daintily and patting a handkerchief against his unstained lips from time to time.

Polyorketes struggled to his feet some two hours later. He swayed a bit, looking like the Spirit of Hangover. He did not try to come closer to Stuart, but spoke from where he stood.

He said, 'You stinking greenie spy, you watch yourself.'

'You heard what I said before, Polyorketes.'

'I heard. But I also heard what you said about Aristides. I won't bother with you, because you're a bag of nothing but noisy air. But wait, someday you'll blow your air in one face too many and it will be let out of you.'

'I'll wait,' said Stuart.

Windham hobbled over, leaning heavily on his cane. 'Now, now,' he called with a wheezing joviality that overlaid his sweating anxiety so thinly as to emphasize it. 'We're all Earthmen, dash it. Got to remember that; keep it as a glowing light of inspiration. Never let down before the blasted Kloros. We've got to forget private feuds and remember only that we are Earthmen united against alien blighters.'

Stuart's comment was unprintable.

Porter was right behind Windham. He had been in a close conference with the shaven-headed colonel for an hour, and now he said with indignation. 'It doesn't help to be a wiseguy, Stuart. You listen to the colonel. We've been doing some hard thinking about the situation.'

He had washed some of the grease off his face, wet his hair and slicked it back. It did not remove the little tic on his right cheek just at the point where his lips ended, or make his hangnail hand more attractive in appearance.

'All right, Colonel,' said Stuart. 'What's on your mind?'

Windham said, 'I'd prefer to have all the men together.'

'Okay, call them.'

Leblanc hurried over; Mullen approached with greater deliberation.

Stuart said, 'You want that fellow?' He jerked his head at Polyorketes.

'Why, yes. Mr. Polyorketes, may we have you, old fella?'

'Ah, leave me alone.'

'Go ahead,' said Stuart, 'leave him alone. I don't want him.'

'No, no,' said Windham. 'This is a matter for all Earthmen. Mr. Polyorketes, we must have you.'

Polyorketes rolled off one side of his cot. 'I'm close enough, I can hear you.'

Windham said to Stuart, 'Would they – the Kloros, I mean – have this room wired?'

'No,' said Stuart. 'Why should they?'

'Are you sure?'

'Of course I'm sure. They didn't know what happened when Polyorketes jumped me. They just heard the thumping when it started rattling the ship.'

'Maybe they were trying to give us the impression the room wasn't wired.'

'Listen, Colonel, I've never known a Kloro to tell a deliberate lie –'

Polyorketes interrupted calmly, 'That lump of noise just *loves* the Kloros.'

Windham said hastily, 'Let's not begin that. Look, Stuart, Porter and I have been discussing matters and we have decided that you know the Kloros well enough to think of some way of getting us back to Earth.'

'It happens that you're wrong. I can't think of any way.'

'Maybe there is some way we can take the ship back from the blasted green fellas,' suggested Windham. 'Some weakness they may have. Dash it, you know what I mean.'

'Tell me, Colonel, what are you after? Your own skin or Earth's welfare?'

'I resent that question. I'll have you know that while I'm as careful of my own life as anyone has a right to be, I'm thinking of Earth primarily. And I think that's true of all of us.'

'Damn right,' said Porter, instantly. Leblanc looked anxious, Polyorketes resentful; and Mullen had no expression at all.

'Good,' said Stuart. 'Of course, I don't think we can take the ship. They're armed and we aren't. But there's this. You know why the Kloros took this ship intact. It's because they need ships. They may be better chemists than Earthmen are, but Earthmen are better astronautical engineers. We have bigger, better and more ships. In fact, if our crew had had a proper respect for military axioms in the first place, they would have blown the ship up as soon as it looked as though the Kloros were going to board.'

Leblanc looked horrified. 'And kill the passengers?'

'Why not? You heard what the good colonel said. Every one of us puts his own lousy little life after Earth's interests. What good are we to Earth alive right now? None at all. What harm will this ship do in Kloro hands? A hell of a lot, probably.'

'Just why,' asked Mullen, 'did our men refuse to blow up the ship? They must have had a reason.'

'They did. It's the firmest tradition of Earth's military men that there must never be an unfavorable ratio of casualties. If we had blown ourselves up, twenty fighting men and seven civilians of Earth would be dead as compared with an enemy casualty total of zero. So what happens? We let them board, kill twenty-eight – I'm sure we killed at least that many – and let them have the ship.'

'Talk, talk, talk,' jeered Polyorketes.

'There's a moral to this,' said Stuart. 'We can't take the ship away from the Kloros. We *might* be able to rush them, though, and keep them busy long enough to allow one of us enough time to short the engines.'

'What?' yelled Porter, and Windham shushed him in fright.

'Short the engines,' Stuart repeated. 'That would destroy the ship, of course, which is what we want to do, isn't it?'

Leblanc's lips were white. 'I don't think that would work.'

'We can't be sure till we try. But what have we to lose by trying?'

'Our lives, damn it!' cried Porter. 'You insane maniac, you're crazy!'

'If I'm a maniac,' said Stuart, 'and insane to boot, then naturally I'm crazy. But just remember that if we lose our lives, which is overwhelmingly probable, we lose nothing of value to Earth;

whereas if we destroy the ship, as we just barely might, we do Earth a lot of good. What patriot would hesitate? Who here would put himself ahead of his world?' He looked about in the silence. 'Surely not you, Colonel Windham?'

Windham coughed tremendously. 'My dear man, that is not the question. There must be a way to save the ship for Earth *without* losing our lives, eh?'

'All right. You name it.'

'Let's all think about it. Now there are only two of the Kloros aboard ship. If one of us could sneak up on them and –'

'How? The rest of the ship's all filled with chlorine. We'd have to wear a spacesuit. Gravity in their part of the ship is hopped up to Kloro level, so whoever is patsy in the deal would be clumping around, metal on metal, slow and heavy. Oh, he could sneak up on them, sure – like a skunk trying to sneak downwind.'

'Then we'll drop it all,' Porter's voice shook. 'Listen, Windham, there's not going to be any destroying the ship. My life means plenty to me and if any of you try anything like that, I'll call the Kloros. I mean it.'

'Well,' said Stuart, 'There's hero number one.'

Leblanc said, 'I want to go back to Earth, but I –'

Mullen interrupted, 'I don't think our chances of destroying the ship are good enough unless –'

'Heroes number two and three. What about you, Polyorketes? You would have the chance of killing two Kloros.'

'I want to kill them with my bare hands,' growled the farmer, his heavy fists writhing. 'On their planet, I will kill dozens.'

'That's a nice safe promise for now. What about you, Colonel? Don't you want to march to death and glory with me?'

'Your attitude is very cynical and unbecoming, Stuart. It's obvious that if the rest are unwilling, then your plan will fall through.'

'Unless I do it myself, huh?'

'You won't, do you hear?' said Porter, instantly.

'Damn right I won't,' agreed Stuart. 'I don't claim to be a hero. I'm just an average patriot, perfectly willing to head for any planet they take me to and sit out the war.'

Mullen said, thoughtfully, 'Of course, there *is* a way we could surprise the Kloros.'

The statement would have dropped flat except for Polyorketes.

He pointed a black-nailed, stubby forefinger and laughed harshly. 'Mr. Bookkeeper!' he said. 'Mr. Bookkeeper, go ahead. You make big speeches also. Let the words roll like an empty barrel.'

He turned to Stuart and repeated venomously, 'Empty barrel! Cripple-hand empty barrel. No good for anything but talk.'

Mullen's soft voice could make no headway until Polyorketes was through, but then he said, speaking directly to Stuart, 'We might be able to reach them from outside. This room has a C-chute I'm sure.'

'What's a C-chute?' asked Leblanc.

'Well –' began Mullen, and then stopped, at a loss.

Stuart said, mockingly, 'It's a euphemism, my boy. Its full name is "casualty chute". It doesn't get talked about, but the main rooms on any ship would have them. They're just little airlocks down which you slide a corpse. Burial at space. Always lots of sentiment and bowed heads, with the captain making a rolling speech of the type Polyorketes here wouldn't like.'

Leblanc's face twisted. 'Use *that* to leave the ship?'

'Why not? Superstitious? – Go on, Mullen.'

The little man had waited patiently. He said, 'Once outside, one could re-enter the ship by the steam-tubes. It can be done – with luck. And then you would be an unexpected visitor in the control room.'

Stuart stared at him curiously. 'How do you figure this out? What do *you* know about steam-tubes?'

Mullen coughed. 'You mean because I'm in the paper-box business? Well –' He grew pink, waited a moment, then made a new start in a colorless, unemotional voice. 'My company, which manufactures fancy paper boxes and novelty containers, made a line of space-ship candy boxes for the juvenile trade some years ago. It was designed so that if a string were pulled, small pressure containers were punctured and jets of compressed air shot out through the mock steam-tubes, sailing the box across the room and scattering candy as it went. The sales theory was that the youngsters would find it exciting to play with the ship and fun to scramble for the candy.

'Actually, it was a complete failure. The ship would break dishes and sometimes hit another child in the eye. Worse still, the children would not only scramble for the candy but would fight over it. It was almost our worst failure. We lost thousands.

'Still, while the boxes were being designed, the entire office was extremely interested. It was like a game, very bad for efficiency and office morale. For a while, we all became steam-tube experts. I read quite a few books on ship construction. On my own time, however, not the company's.'

Stuart was intrigued. He said, 'You know it's a video sort of idea, but it might work if we had a hero to spare. Have we?'

'What about you?' demanded Porter, indignantly. 'You go around sneering at us with your cheap wisecracks. I don't notice you volunteering for anything.'

'That's because I'm no hero, Porter. I admit it. My object is to stay alive. But the rest of you are noble patriots. The colonel says so. What about you, Colonel? You're the senior hero here.'

Windham said, 'If I were younger, blast it, and if you had your hands, I would take pleasure, sir, in trouncing you soundly.'

'I've no doubt of it, but that's no answer.'

'You know very well that at my time of life and with my leg –' he brought the flat of his hand down upon his stiff knee – 'I am in no position to do anything of the sort, however much I should wish to.'

'Ah, yes,' said Stuart, 'and I, myself, am crippled in the hands, as Polyorketes tells me. That saves us. And what unfortunate deformities do the rest of us have?'

'Listen,' cried Porter, 'I want to know what this is all about. How can anyone go down the steam-tubes? What if the Kloros use them while one of us is inside?'

'Why, Porter, that's part of the sporting chance. It's where the excitement comes in.'

'But he'd be boiled in the shell like a lobster.'

'A pretty image, but inaccurate. The steam wouldn't be on for more than a very short time, maybe a second or two, and the suit insulation would hold that long. Besides, the jet comes scooting out at several hundred miles a minute, so that you would be blown clear of the ship before the steam could even warm you. In fact, you'd be blown quite a few miles out into space, and after that you would be quite safe from the Kloros. Of course, you couldn't get back to the ship.'

Porter was sweating freely. 'You don't scare me for one minute, Stuart.'

'I don't? Then you're offering to go? Are you sure you've thought out what being stranded in space means? You're all alone, you know; really all alone. The steam-jet will probably leave you turning or tumbling pretty rapidly. You won't feel that. You'll seem to be motionless. But all the stars will be going around and around so that they're just streaks in the sky. They won't ever stop. They won't even slow up. Then your heater will go off, your oxygen will give out, and you will die very slowly. You'll have lots of time to think. Or, if you are in a hurry, you could open your suit. That wouldn't be pleasant, either. I've seen faces of men who had a torn suit happen to them accidentally, and it's pretty awful. But it would be quicker. Then —'

Porter turned and walked unsteadily away.

Stuart said, lightly, 'Another failure. One act of heroism still ready to be knocked down to the highest bidder with nothing offered yet.'

Polyorketes spoke up and his harsh voice roughed the words. 'You keep on talking, Mr. Big Mouth. You just keep banging that empty barrel. Pretty soon, we'll kick your teeth in. There's one boy I think would be willing to do it now, eh, Mr. Porter?'

Porter's look at Stuart confirmed the truth of Polyorketes' remarks, but he said nothing.

Stuart said, 'Then what about you, Polyorketes? You're the bare-hand man with guts. Want me to help you into a suit?'

'I'll ask you when I want help.'

'What about you, Leblanc?'

The young man shrank away.

'Not even to get back to Margaret?'

But Leblanc could only shake his head.

'Mullen?'

'Well — I'll try.'

'You'll what?'

'I said, yes, I'll try. After all, it's my idea.'

Stuart looked stunned. 'You're serious? How come?'

Mullen's prim mouth pursed. 'Because no one else will.'

'But that's no reason. Especially for you.'

Mullen shrugged.

There was a thump of a cane behind Stuart. Windham brushed past.

He said, 'Do you really intend to go, Mullen?'

'Yes, Colonel.'

'In that case, dash it, let me shake your hand. I like you. You're an — an Earthman, by heaven. Do this, and win or die, I'll bear witness for you.'

Mullen withdrew his hand awkwardly from the deep and vibrating grasp of the other.

And Stuart just stood there. He was in a very unusual position. He was, in fact, in the particular position of all positions in which he most rarely found himself.

He had nothing to say.

The quality of tension had changed. The gloom and frustration had lifted a bit, and the excitement of conspiracy had replaced it. Even Polyorketes was fingering the spacesuits and commenting briefly and hoarsely on which he considered preferable.

Mullen was having a certain amount of trouble. The suit hung rather limply upon him even though the adjustable joints had been tightened nearly to a minimum. He stood there now with only the helmet to be screwed on. He wiggled his neck.

Stuart was holding the helmet with an effort. It was heavy, and his artiplasmic hands did not grip it well. He said, 'Better scratch your nose if it itches. It's your last chance for a while.' He didn't add, 'Maybe forever,' but he thought it.

Mullen said, tonelessly, 'I think perhaps I had better have a spare oxygen cylinder.'

'Good enough.'

'With a reducing valve.'

Stuart nodded. 'I see what you're thinking of. If you do get blown clear of the ship, you could try to blow yourself back by using the cylinder as an action-reaction motor.'

They clamped on the headpiece and buckled the spare cylinder to Mullen's waist. Polyorketes and Leblanc lifted him up to the yawning opening of the C-tube. It was ominously dark inside, the metal lining of the interior having been painted a mournful black. Stuart thought he could detect a musty odor about it, but that, he knew, was only imagination.

He stopped the proceedings when Mullen was half within the tube. He tapped upon the little man's faceplate.

'Can you hear me?'

Within, there was a nod.

'Air coming through all right? No last-minute troubles?'

Mullen lifted his armored arm in a gesture of reassurance.

'Then remember, don't use the suit-radio out there. The Kloros might pick up the signals.'

Reluctantly, he stepped away. Polyorketes' brawny hands lowered Mullen until they could hear the thumping sound made by the steel-shod feet against the outer valve. The inner valve then swung shut with a dreadful finality, its beveled silicone gasket making a slight soughing noise as it crushed hard. They clamped it into place.

Stuart stood at the toggle-switch that controlled the outer valve. He threw it and the gauge that marked the air pressure within the tube fell to zero. A little pinpoint of red light warned that the outer valve was open. Then the light disappeared, the valve closed, and the gauge climbed slowly to fifteen pounds again.

They opened the inner valve again and found the tube empty.

Polyorketes spoke first. He said, 'The little son-of-a-gun. He went!' He looked wonderingly at the others. 'A little fellow with guts like that.'

Stuart said, 'Look, we'd better get ready in here. There's just a chance that the Kloros may have detected the valves opening and closing. If so, they'll be here to investigate and we'll have to cover up.'

'How?' asked Windham.

'They won't see Mullen anywhere around. We'll say he's in the head. The Kloros know that it's one of the peculiar characteristics of Earthmen that they resent intrusion on their privacy in lavatories, and they'll make no effort to check. If we can hold them off –'

'What if they wait, or if they check the spacesuits?' asked Porter.

Stuart shrugged. 'Let's hope they don't. And listen, Polyorketes, don't make any fuss when they come in.'

Polyorketes grunted, 'With that little guy out there? What do you think I am?' He stared at Stuart without animosity, then scratched his curly hair vigorously. 'You know, I laughed at him. I thought he was an old woman. It makes me ashamed.'

Stuart cleared his throat. He said, 'Look, I've been saying some things that maybe weren't too funny after all, now that I come to think of it. I'd like to say I'm sorry if I have.'

He turned away morosely and walked toward his cot. He heard the steps behind him, felt the touch on his sleeve. He turned; it was Leblanc.

The youngster said softly, 'I keep thinking that Mr. Mullen is an old man.'

'Well, he's not a kid. He's about forty-five or fifty, I think.'

Leblanc said, 'Do you think, Mr. Stuart, that *I* should have gone, instead? I'm the youngest here. I don't like the thought of having let an old man go in my place. It makes me feel like the devil.'

'I know. If he dies, it will be too bad.'

'But he volunteered. We didn't make him, did we?'

'Don't try to dodge responsibility, Leblanc. It won't make you feel better. There isn't one of us without a stronger motive to run the risk than he had.' And Stuart sat there silently, thinking.

Mullen felt the obstruction beneath his feet yield and the walls about him slip away quickly, too quickly. He knew it was the puff of air escaping, carrying him with it, and he dug arms and legs frantically against the wall to brake himself. Corpses were supposed to be flung well clear of the ship, but he was no corpse – for the moment.

His feet swung free and threshed. He heard the *clunk* of one magnetic boot against the hull just as the rest of his body puffed out like a tight cork under air pressure. He teetered dangerously at the lip of the hole in the ship – he had changed orientation suddenly and was looking down on it – then took a step backward as its lid came down of itself and fitted smoothly against the hull.

A feeling of unreality overwhelmed him. Surely, it wasn't he standing on the outer surface of a ship. Not Randolph F. Mullen. So few human beings could ever say they had, even those who traveled in space constantly.

He was only gradually aware that he was in pain. Popping out of that hole with one foot clamped to the hull had nearly bent him in two. He tried moving, cautiously, and found his motions to be erratic and almost impossible to control. He *thought* nothing was broken, though the muscles of his left side were badly wrenched.

And then he came to himself and noticed that the wrist-lights of his suit were on. It was by their light that he had stared into the blackness of the C-chute. He stirred with the nervous thought that from within, the Kloros might see the twin spots of moving light just outside the hull. He flicked the switch upon the suit's mid-section.

Mullen had never imagined that, standing on a ship, he would fail to see its hull. But it was dark, as dark below as above. There were the stars, hard and bright little non-dimensional dots. Nothing more. Nothing more anywhere. Under his feet, not even the stars – *not even his feet*.

He bent back to look at the stars. His head swam. They were moving slowly. Or, rather, they were standing still and the ship was rotating, but he could not tell his eyes that. *They* moved. His eyes followed – down and behind the ship. New stars up and above from the other side. A black horizon. The ship existed only as a region where there were no stars.

No stars? Why, there was one almost at his feet. He nearly reached for it; then he realized that it was only a glittering reflection in the mirroring metal.

They were moving thousand of miles an hour. The stars were. The ship was. He was. But it meant nothing. To his senses, there was only silence and darkness and that slow wheeling of the stars. His eyes followed the wheeling –

And his head in its helmet hit the ship's hull with a soft bell-like ring.

He felt about in panic with his thick, insensitive, spun-silicate gloves. His feet were still firmly magnetized to the hull, that was true, but the rest of his body bent backward at the knees in a right angle. There was no gravity outside the ship. If he bent back, there was nothing to pull the upper part of his body down and tell his joints they were bending. His body stayed as he put it.

He pressed wildly against the hull and his torso shot upward and refused to stop when upright. He fell forward.

He tried more slowly, balancing with both hands against the hull, until he squatted evenly. Then upward. Very slowly. Straight up. Arms out to balance.

He was straight now, aware of his nausea and lightheadedness.

He looked about. My God, where were the steam-tubes? He couldn't see them. They were black on black, nothing on nothing.

Quickly, he turned on the wrist-lights. In space, there were no beams, only elliptical, sharply defined spots of blue steel, winking light back at him. Where they struck a rivet, a shadow was cast, knife-sharp and as black as space, the lighted region illuminated abruptly and without diffusion.

He moved his arms, his body swaying gently in the opposite direction; action and reaction. The vision of a steam-tube with its smooth cylindrical sides sprang at him.

He tried to move toward it. His foot held firmly to the hull. He pulled and it slogged upward, straining against quicksand that eased quickly. Three inches up and it had almost sucked free; six inches up and he thought it would fly away.

He advanced it and let it down, felt it enter the quicksand. When the sole was within two inches of the hull, it snapped down; out of control, hitting the hull ringingly. His spacesuit carried the vibrations, amplifying them in his ears.

He stopped in absolute terror. The dehydrators that dried the atmosphere within his suit could not handle the sudden gush of perspiration that drenched his forehead and armpits.

He waited, then tried lifting his foot again – a bare inch, holding it there by main force and moving it horizontally. Horizontal motion involved no effort at all; it was motion perpendicular to the lines of magnetic force. But he had to keep his foot from snapping down as he did so, and then lower it slowly.

He puffed with the effort. Each step was agony. The tendons of his knees were cracking, and there were knives in his side.

Mullen stopped to let the perspiration dry. It wouldn't do to steam up the inside of his faceplate. He flashed his wrist-lights, and the steam-cylinder was right ahead.

The ship had four of them, at ninety degree intervals, thrusting out at an angle from the midgirdle. They were the 'fine adjustment' of the ship's course. The coarse adjustment was the powerful thrusters back and front which fixed final velocity by their accelerative and the decelerative force, and the hyperatomics that took care of the space-swallowing Jumps.

But occasionally the direction of flight had to be adjusted slightly and then the steam-cylinders took over. Singly, they could drive the ship up, down, right, left. By twos, in appropriate ratios of thrust, the ship could be turned in any desired direction.

The device had been unimproved in centuries, being too simple to improve. The atomic pile heated the water content of a closed container into steam, driving it, in less than a second, up to temperatures where it would have broken down into a mixture of hydrogen and oxygen, and then into a mixture of electrons and ions. Perhaps the breakdown actually took place. No one ever bothered testing; it worked, so there was no need to.

At the critical point, a needle valve gave way and the steam thrust madly out in a short but incredible blast. And the ship, inevitably and majestically, moved in the opposite direction, veering about its own center of gravity. When the degrees of turn were sufficient, an equal and opposite blast would take place and the turning would be canceled. The ship would be moving at its original velocity, but in a new direction.

Mullen had dragged himself out to the lip of the steam-cylinder. He had a picture of himself – a small speck teetering at the extreme end of a structure thrusting out of an ovoid that was tearing through space at ten thousand miles an hour.

But there was no air-stream to whip him off the hull, and his magnetic soles held him more firmly than he liked.

With lights on, he bent down to peer into the tube and the ship dropped down precipitously as his orientation changed. He reached out to steady himself, but he was not falling. There was no up or down in space except for what his confused mind chose to consider up or down.

The cylinder was just large enough to hold a man, so that it might be entered for repair purposes. His light caught the rungs almost directly opposite his position at the lip. He puffed a sigh of relief with what breath he could muster. Some ships didn't have ladders.

He made his way to it, the ship appearing to slip and twist beneath him as he moved. He lifted an arm over the lip of the tube, feeling for the rung, loosened each foot, and drew himself within.

The knot in his stomach that had been there from the first was a convulsed agony now. If they should choose to manipulate the ship, if the steam should whistle out now –

He would never hear it; never know it. One instant he would be holding a rung, feeling slowly for the next with a groping arm. The next moment he would be alone in space, the ship a dark, dark nothingness lost forever among the stars. There would be, perhaps, a brief glory of swirling ice crystals drifting with him, shining in his wrist-lights and slowly approaching and rotating about him, attracted by his mass like infinitesimal planets to an absurdly tiny Sun.

He was trickling sweat again, and now he was also conscious of thirst. He put it out of his mind. There would be no drinking until he was out of his suit – if ever.

Up a rung; up another; and another. How many were there? His hand slipped and he stared in disbelief at the glitter that showed under his light.

Ice?

Why not? The steam, incredibly hot as it was, would strike metal that was at nearly absolute zero. In the few split-seconds of thrust, there would not be time for the metal to warm above the freezing point of water. A sheet of ice would condense that would sublime slowly into the vacuum. It was the speed of all that happened that prevented the fusion of the tubes and of the original water-container itself.

His groping hand reached the end. Again the wrist-lights. He stared with crawling horror at the steam nozzle, half an inch in diameter. It looked dead, harmless. But it always would, right up to the micro-second before –

Around it was the outer steam lock. It pivoted on a central hub that was springed on the portion toward space, screwed on the part toward the ship. The springs allowed it to give under the first wild thrust of steam pressure before the ship's mighty inertia could be overcome. The steam was bled into the inner chamber, breaking the force of the thrust, leaving the total energy unchanged, but spreading it over time so that the hull itself was in that much less danger of being staved in.

Mullen braced himself firmly against a rung and pressed against the outer lock so that it gave a little. It was stiff, but it didn't have to give much, just enough to catch on the screw. He felt it catch.

He strained against it and turned it, feeling his body twist in the opposite direction. It held tight, the screw taking up the strain as he carefully adjusted the small control switch that allowed the springs to fall free. How well he remembered the books he had read!

He was in the interlock space now, which was large enough to hold a man comfortably, again for convenience in repairs. He could no longer be blown away from the ship. If the steam blast were turned on now, it would merely drive him against the inner lock – hard enough to crush him to a pulp. A quick death he would never feel, at least.

Slowly, he unhooked his spare oxygen cylinder. There was only an inner lock between himself and the control room now. This lock opened outward into space so that the steam blast could only close it tighter, rather than blow it open. And it fitted tightly and smoothly. There was absolutely no way to open it from without.

He lifted himself above the lock, forcing his bent back against the inner surface of the interlock area. It made breathing difficult. The spare oxygen cylinder dangled at a queer angle. He held its metal-mesh hose and straightened it, forcing it against the inner lock so that vibration thudded. Again – again –

It would *have* to attract the attention of the Kloros. They would *have* to investigate.

He would have no way of telling when they were about to do so. Ordinarily, they would first let air into the interlock to force the outer lock shut. But now the outer lock was on the central screw, well away from its rim. Air would suck about it ineffectually, dragging out into space.

Mullen kept on thumping. Would the Kloros look at the air-gauge, note that it scarcely lifted from zero, or would they take its proper working for granted?

Porter said, 'He's been gone an hour and a half.'

'I know,' said Stuart.

They were all restless, jumpy, but the tension among themselves had disappeared. It was as though all the threads of emotion extended to the hull of the ship.

Porter was bothered. His philosophy of life had always been simple – take care of yourself because no one will take care of you for you. It upset him to see it shaken.

He said, 'Do you suppose they've caught him?'

'If they had, we'd hear about it,' replied Stuart, briefly.

Porter felt, with a miserable twinge, that there was little interest on the part of the others in speaking to him. He could understand it; he had not exactly earned their respect. For the moment, a torrent of self-excuse poured through his mind. The others had been frightened, too. A man had a right to be afraid. No one likes to die. At least, he hadn't broken like Aristides Polyorketes. He hadn't wept like Leblanc. He –

But there was Mullen, out there on the hull.

'Listen,' he cried, 'why did he do it?' They turned to look at him, not understanding, but Porter didn't care. It bothered him to the point where it had to come out. 'I want to know why Mullen is risking his life.'

'The man', said Windham, 'is a patriot –'

'No, none of that!' Porter was almost hysterical. 'That little fellow has no emotions at all. He just has reasons and I want to know what those reasons are, because –'

He didn't finish the sentence. Could he say that if those reasons applied to a little middle-aged bookkeeper, they might apply even more forcibly to himself?

Polyorketes said, 'He's one brave damn little fellow.'

Porter got to his feet. 'Listen,' he said, 'he may be stuck out there. Whatever he's doing, he may not be able to finish it alone. I – I volunteer to go out after him.'

He was shaking as he said it and he waited in fear for the sarcastic lash of Stuart's tongue. Stuart was staring at him, probably with surprise, but Porter dared not meet his eyes to make certain.

Stuart said, mildly, 'Let's give him another half-hour.'

Porter looked up, startled. There was no sneer on Stuart's face. It was even friendly. They all looked friendly.

He said, 'And then –'

'And then all those who do volunteer will draw straws or something equally democratic. Who volunteers, besides Porter?'

They all raised their hands; Stuart did, too.

But Porter was happy. He had volunteered first. He was anxious for the half-hour to pass.

It caught Mullen by surprise. The outer lock flew open and the long, thin, snakelike, almost headless neck of a Kloro sucked out, unable to fight the blast of escaping air.

Mullen's cylinder flew away, almost tore free. After one wild moment of frozen panic, he fought for it, dragging it above the air-stream, waiting as long as he dared to let the first fury die down as the air of the control room thinned out, then bringing it down with force.

It caught the sinewy neck squarely, crushing it. Mullen, curled above the lock, almost entirely protected from the stream, raised the cylinder again and plunging it down again striking the head, mashing the staring eyes to liquid ruin. In the near-vacuum, green blood was pumping out of what was left of the neck.

Mullen dared not vomit, but he wanted to.

With eyes averted, he backed away, caught the outer lock with one hand and imparted a whirl. For several seconds, it maintained that whirl. At the end of the screw, the springs engaged automatically and pulled it shut. What was left of the atmosphere tightened it and the laboring pumps could now begin to fill the control room once again.

Mullen crawled over the mangled Kloro and into the room. It was empty.

He had barely time to notice that when he found himself on his knees. He rose with difficulty. the transition from non-gravity to gravity had taken him entirely by surprise. It was Klorian gravity, too, which meant that with this suit, he carried a fifty per cent overload for his small frame. At least, though, his heavy metal clogs no longer clung so exasperatingly to the metal underneath. Within the ship, floors and wall were of cork-covered aluminium alloy.

He circled slowly. The neckless Kloro had collapsed and lay with only an occasional twitch to show it had once been a living organism. He stepped over it, distastefully, and drew the steam-tube lock shut.

The room had a depressing bilious cast and the lights shone yellow-green. It was the Kloro atmosphere, of course.

Mullen felt a twinge of surprise and reluctant admiration. The Kloros obviously had some way of treating materials so that they were impervious to the oxidizing effect of chlorine. Even the map of Earth on the wall, printed on glossy plastic-backed paper, seemed fresh and untouched. He approached, drawn by the familiar outlines of the continents –

There was a flash of motion caught in the corner of his eyes. As quickly as he could in his heavy suit, he turned, then screamed. The Kloro he had thought dead was rising to its feet.

Its neck hung limp, an oozing mass of tissue mash, but its arms reached out blindly, and the tentacles about its chest vibrated rapidly like innumerable snakes' tongues.

It was blind, of course. The destruction of its neck-stalk had deprived it of all sensory equipment, and partial asphyxiation had disorganized it. But the brain remained whole and safe in the abdomen. It still lived.

Mullen backed away. He circled, trying clumsily and unsuccessfully to tiptoe, though he knew that what was left of the Kloro was also deaf. It blundered on its way, struck a wall, felt to the base and began sidling along it.

Mullen cast about desperately for a weapon, found nothing.

There was the Kloro's holster, but he dared not reach for it. Why hadn't he snatched it at the very first? Fool!

The door to the control room opened. It made almost no noise. Mullen turned, quivering.

The other Kloro entered, unharmed, entire. It stood in the doorway for a moment, chest-tendrils stiff and unmoving; its neck-stalk stretched forward; its horrible eyes flickering first at him and then at its nearly dead comrade.

And then its hand moved quickly to its side.

Mullen, without awareness, moved as quickly in pure reflex. He stretched out the hose of the spare oxygen-cylinder, which, since entering the control room, he had replaced in its suit-clamp, and cracked the valve. He didn't bother reducing the pressure. He let it gush out unchecked so that he nearly staggered under the backward push.

He could *see* the oxygen stream. It was a pale puff, billowing out amid the chlorine-green. It caught the Kloro with one hand on the weapon's holster.

The Kloro threw its hands up. The little beak on its head-nodule opened alarmingly but noiselessly. It staggered and fell, writhed for a moment, then lay still. Mullen approached and played the oxygen-stream upon its body as though he were extinguishing a fire. And then he raised his heavy foot and brought it down upon the center of the neck-stalk and crushed it on the floor.

He turned to the first. It was sprawled, rigid.

The whole room was pale with oxygen, enough to kill whole legions of Kloros, and his cylinder was empty.

Mullen stepped over the dead Kloro, out of the control room and along the main corridor toward the prisoners' room.

Reaction had set in. He was whimpering in blind, incoherent fright.

Stuart was tired. False hands and all, he was at the controls of a ship once again. Two light cruisers of Earth were on the way. For better than twenty-four hours he had handled the controls virtually alone. He had discarded the chlorinating equipment, rerigged the old atmospherics, located the ship's position in space, tried to plot a course, and sent out carefully guarded signals – which had worked.

So when the door of the control room opened, he was a little annoyed. He was too tired to play conversational handball. Then he turned, and it was Mullen stepping inside.

Stuart said, 'For God's sake, get back into bed, Mullen!'

Mullen said, 'I'm tired of sleeping, even though I never thought I would be a while ago.'

'How do you feel?'

'I'm stiff all over. Especially my side.' He grimaced and stared involuntarily around.

'Don't look for the Kloros,' Stuart said. 'We dumped the poor devils.' He shook his head. 'I was sorry for them. To themselves, *they're* the human beings, you know, and *we're* the aliens. Not that I'd rather they'd killed you, you understand.'

'I understand.'

Stuart turned a sidelong glance upon the little man who sat looking at the map of Earth and went on, 'I owe you a particular and personal apology, Mullen. I didn't think much of you.'

'It was your privilege,' said Mullen in his dry voice. There was no feeling in it.

'No, it wasn't. It is no one's privilege to despise another. It is only a hard-won right after long experience.'

'Have you been thinking about this?'

'Yes, all day. Maybe I can't explain. It's these hands.' He held them up before him, spread out. 'It was hard knowing that other people had hands of their own. I had to hate them for it. I always had to do my best to investigate and belittle their motives, point up their deficiencies, expose their stupidities. I had to do anything that would prove to myself that they weren't worth envying.'

Mullen moved restlessly. 'This explanation is not necessary.'

'It is. It is!' Stuart felt his thoughts intently, strained to put them into words. 'For years I've abandoned hope of finding any decency in human beings. Then you climbed into the C-chute.'

'You had better understand', said Mullen, 'that I was motivated by practical and selfish considerations. I will not have you present me to myself as a hero.'

'I wasn't intending to. I know that you would do nothing without a reason. It was what your action did to the rest of us. It turned a collection of phonies and fools into decent people. And not by magic either. They were decent all along. It was just that they needed something to live up to and you supplied it. And – I'm one of them. I'll have to live up to you, too. For the rest of my life, probably.'

Mullen turned away uncomfortably. His hand straightened his sleeves, which were not in the least twisted. His finger rested on the map.

He said, 'I was born in Richmond, Virginia, you know. Here it is. I'll be going there first. Where were you born?'

'Toronto,' said Stuart.

'That's right here. Not very far apart on the map, is it?'

Stuart said, 'Would you tell me something?'

'If I can.'

'Just why *did* you go out there?'

Mullen's precise mouth pursed. He said, dryly, 'Wouldn't my rather prosaic reason ruin the inspirational effect?'

'Call it intellectual curiosity. Each of the rest of us had such obvious motives. Porter was scared to death of being interned; Leblanc wanted to get back to his sweetheart; Polyorketes wanted to kill Kloros; and Windham was a patriot according to his lights. As for me, I thought of myself as a noble idealist, I'm afraid. Yet in none of us was the motivation strong enough to get us into a spacesuit and out the C-chute. Then what made *you* do it, *you*, of all people?'

'Why the phrase, "of all people"?'

'Don't be offended, but you seem devoid of all emotion.'

'Do I?' Mullen's voice did not change. It remained precise and soft, yet somehow a tightness had entered it. 'That's only training, Mr. Stuart, and self-discipline; not nature. A small man can have no respectable emotions. Is there anything more ridiculous than a man like myself in a state of rage? I'm five feet and one-half inch tall, and one hundred and two pounds in weight, if you care for exact figures. I insist on the half inch and the two pounds.

'Can I be dignified? Proud? Draw myself to my full height without inducing laughter? Where can I meet a woman who will not dismiss me instantly with a giggle? Naturally, I've had to learn to dispense with external display of emotion.

'*You* talk about deformities. No one would notice your hands or know they were different, if you weren't so eager to tell people all about it the instant you meet them. Do you think that the eight inches of height I do not have can be hidden? That it is not the first and, in most cases, the only thing about me that a person will notice?'

Stuart was ashamed. He had invaded a privacy he ought not to have. He said, 'I'm sorry.'

'Why?'

'I should not have forced you to speak of this. I should have seen for myself that you – that you –'

'That I what? Tried to prove myself? Tried to show that while I might be small in body, I held within it a giant's heart?'

'I would not have put it mockingly.'

'Why not? It's a foolish idea, and nothing like it is the reason I did what I did. What would I have accomplished if that's what was in my mind? Will they take me to Earth now and put me up before the television cameras – pitching them low, of course, to catch my face, or standing me on a chair – and pin medals on me?'

'They are quite likely to do exactly that.'

'And what good would it do me? They would say, "Gee, and he's such a little guy." And afterward, what? Shall I tell each man I meet, "You know, I'm the fellow they decorated for incredible valor last month?" How many medals, Mr. Stuart, do you suppose it would take to put eight inches and sixty pounds on me?'

Stuart said, 'Put that way, I see your point.'

Mullen was speaking a trifle more quickly now; a controlled heat had entered his words, warming them to just a tepid room temperature. 'There *were* days when I thought I would show them, the mysterious "them" that includes all the world. I was going to leave Earth and carve out worlds for myself. I would be a new and even smaller Napoleon. So I left Earth and went to Arcturus. And what could I do on Arcturus that I could not have done on Earth? Nothing. I balance books. So I am past the vanity, Mr. Stuart, of trying to stand on tiptoe.'

'Then why *did* you do it?'

'I left Earth when I was twenty-eight and came to the Arcturian System. I've been there ever since. This trip was to be my first vacation, my first visit back to Earth in all that time. I was going to stay on Earth for six months. The Kloros instead captured us and would have kept us interned indefinitely. But I couldn't – I *couldn't* let them stop me from traveling to Earth. No matter what the risk, I had to prevent their interference. It

wasn't love of woman, or fear, or hate, or idealism of any sort.
It was stronger than any of those.'

He stopped, and stretched out a hand as though to caress the
map on the wall.

'Mr. Stuart,' Mullen asked quietly, 'haven't you ever been
homesick?'